Protecting His Pet

Measha Stone

Published by Stormy Night Publications and Design, LLC.
www.StormyNightPublications.com

Cover design by Korey Mae Johnson
www.koreymaejohnson.com

Images by RomanceNovelsCovers/Jimmy Thomas and
123RF/Andrey Alyukhin

1st Print Edition. January 2017

ISBN-13: 978-1542861731

ISBN-10: 154286173X

FOR AUDIENCES 18+ ONLY

This book is intended for adults only. Spanking and other sexual activities represented in this book are fantasies only, intended for adults.

CHAPTER ONE

The busses were running late again. No big surprise, especially in the middle of September on a day the Cubs played at home. The game having just let out within the hour, the Addison route would be packed with half drunk or totally drunk fans making their way home.

Kara tilted her chin up into the soft wind of fall, delighting in the slight chill. The heat and humidity of Chicago summer had finally broken, leaving a more habitable environment. She hated heat above all else.

"Did we miss it?" Julie jogged up to her at the bus stop, breath heaving from the exertion.

Kara laughed. "No, it's late. And will be crowded as hell, too."

"I know. Damn those emergencies." Julie pulled a pack of cigarettes from her scrub pocket and dug out a fresh smoke. Kara watched Julie light the cigarette then blow a large cloud into the air before stuffing her pack and lighter back into her pocket. "I was hoping to get out before the game ended."

Kara looked down the street, past the line of cars waiting to get through the traffic light in hopes of sighting the bus. The eye clinic they worked at stayed open later for an emergency chemical burn, making them miss the last bus before the Cubs game destroyed traffic. "It's times like this that I wish I owned a car." Kara gave up trying to find the green limousine and plunked down on the bench. She sat in front of the latest photograph of the top realtor in the area.

"In the city? And where would you park it?" Julie scoffed. It was true. Parking spots were a commodity that her medical receptionist salary couldn't cover, even in her supervisory role. "You know, you could have left. I was there, so was Dr. Conrad; you didn't need to stay."

"Someone needed to check the guy out and make his next appointment. I wasn't going to leave that up to you. You technicians mess up the schedule whenever you touch it." Julie looked at her, one eyebrow raised over the edge of the sunglasses perched high on her nose. Kara wouldn't let anyone else handle what she considered to be her responsibility, and they both knew it. If it needed doing, she'd get it done. Leaving while there was still a patient in the office wasn't going to happen. She'd expect any of the receptionists beneath her to stay until the patient had been fully checked out, and she wouldn't do less than she expected of her subordinates.

A black sedan pulled in front of Kara and she sighed. She hadn't called him, so of course he'd come to her work looking for her.

"My brother." Kara waved at the car in explanation. "I forgot to text him, it's our dinner night." She waved to Tommy, who gave a curt nod and started playing with his phone.

Julie ducked a bit to look in the window. "He's sorta cute," she said, sucking in a drag of her cigarette.

"No, he's not," Kara corrected. "He's my brother. He's obnoxious… I'll see you tomorrow." Kara pulled open the passenger door and climbed into the front seat, dumping her purse between her legs before snapping on her seat belt. Tommy had already pulled into traffic before she could adjust the belt.

"You didn't call or text," he said, flipping the radio off and checking his mirrors. First the side views, then the rearview.

"Had an emergency, and I was cleaning up. I forgot." She leaned her head back against the headrest. "So, pizza or you wanna go back to my place?"

Tommy checked the mirrors again then gave her a look that suggested she knew better than to think they'd go to her place. "Pizza's good. Here, order it now and it will be there by the time we get to my place." Tommy tossed her his phone. Tommy had a specific preference for every one of his take-outs, and all were programmed in his phone.

"Cheese okay?" she asked as she hit the pizza contact in his directory.

"Yeah, yeah, that's fine," he nodded, checking the mirrors again.

"You seem more tense than usual." She tried to laugh, but the muscles in his neck were strung pretty tight and if he checked those damn mirrors again, she'd lose her mind.

He let out a long breath. "Don't start, okay? Everything's fine."

After placing the order, she clicked off the call, noticing the messages in his text screen that he had left up. She quickly ran through them, her stomach clenching. The code left her mostly in the dark, because most people didn't talk in code. People with normal jobs didn't need to do that, they just said what they wanted to say. She put the phone back in the middle console.

"Don't worry, Kara." He patted her knee. "It's fine." He'd used the same tone and words when their mom died. She'd been ten, and things were not fine. Not then, and not now.

"Did you apply for that job I emailed you?" She tucked her hair behind her ear.

He sighed and changed lanes. "No. Kara. I told you, I have it covered. Everything's fine. I have some cash for you, too. I know you need some new shit—at least some new shoes; look at those things, they're beat to hell." He pulled up to a stoplight and pointed at her feet. The once-white gym shoes were scuffed and worn, the sole on the right foot was being held together by nearly an entire bottle of superglue, but that didn't change things. She wouldn't take his money.

"Where'd you get the cash?" she asked pointedly.

He smiled at her, the soft smile he always threw her way when he was about to lie. That little tell had been around her entire life. She wasn't a sucker for it anymore. Not when he swore he didn't steal that car so their mom would have a way of getting to work without taking two busses and a train, not when he said he'd borrowed the cash from the guy next door so Kara could get a new bike, and not when he promised her he stopped doing illegal jobs to earn his cash.

"Kara, we've been over this." He pulled his car into the garage behind his apartment building and turned off the ignition.

"Why can't we go to my place? You've never even been to my apartment."

"Because. It's not safe for me to be seen there," he said and popped his door open.

"How can this be the life you want to live, Tommy?" She slammed her door and met him at the garage entrance.

He wrapped a single arm around her shoulder and pulled her close, pressing a kiss to her forehead. "Kara, it's the only way I know how. Now, no more. Let's get the pizza and chow down. Devin's supposed to be here in a couple hours, and I'd rather you be gone before he shows."

"Devin?" She gave him a half smile. She'd met him once before, briefly. A quick hello as she left Tommy's apartment, but she'd seen enough. He was cute—no, that wasn't the word. Hot. Yes, that better described him. Hot.

"He works with me, Kara." The warning in Tommy's voice didn't escape her notice. She didn't need it anyway. If he worked with Tommy, she wouldn't go near him.

"Fine." She shoved her purse strap over her shoulder

and walked down the gangway toward the building. She heard Tommy pick up a call on his cell from behind her. She rolled her eyes and headed up the stairs to his apartment.

The door behind her shut. Loud. She paused on the steps to see if Tommy would open the door. Nothing. She looked out the frosted glass, but couldn't see anything. No shadowed figures, nothing. Her heart started to pound. "It's fine. Just the wind," she promised herself as she turned the knob on the door and slowly pulled it toward her.

Peeking her head out, she looked back down the gangway. No Tommy. She looked the other way, toward the front yard; not a soul. Cars sped down the street, a horn blared from the alley, but nothing from her brother. She stepped down into the small walkway between his building and the next. Her breath caught in her chest, her hand flew to her already trembling lips.

A pool of blood a few feet in front of her, followed by a trail of it going all the way to the alley. She ran, not thinking, to the alley. More blood, but it stopped right at the back gate. Tire marks, black tire marks ran off down the alley.

CHAPTER TWO

Kara padded across her living room in bare feet, wearing her pajama shorts and a tank top. The summer heat may have finally broke, but her garden apartment still wouldn't cool down enough for her to be comfortable.

Google loaded up on her laptop, and she pulled it into her lap. Michigan. Tommy wanted her to drive up to Michigan. She knew she should forget all about the promise he forced out of her years ago, but how could she? Whatever it was that waited for her there had been put there by Tommy, her brother. Her tortured and murdered brother.

Cash. There would be cash; that much she had figured out by his cryptic answers. "*If I get arrested, or go missing, you go up there, Kara. You go and get what's in that box. You got me? You go get it.*" At the time it wasn't his words that concerned her, but the way his eyes widened and darkened when he pleaded with her. The grip he had on her arm had left a bruise behind. She promised him, swore she'd make the trip. He wouldn't tell her anything else, though after pressing him as she always did when he wouldn't cooperate, he tousled her hair like she was still five years old and left.

How much cash was the mystery. Enough for legal representation in the event he was arrested. Whatever shit he had been doing to earn money wasn't legal. Couldn't be. The cops tried to convince her that his death was just a drug deal gone bad. He owed a dealer probably, they tried to tell her, but Tommy didn't do drugs. They wouldn't listen. No one cared.

Looking at the map again, she figured she could either rent a car or take the bus up to Michigan. The bus might be cheaper, but it would take longer. She only had the weekend. Leave on Friday night, home by Sunday night in time for her Monday shift at the eye clinic.

Normally, the idea of tracking down a suitcase of money wouldn't enter her mind. But Tommy didn't exactly have a life insurance policy, and funerals—even the most modest—were expensive. Her bank account couldn't sit out the drought much longer.

Kara decided on a rental, clicked over to a new web page, and made the reservation. Her phone buzzed a few times on the coffee table, but she ignored it. Julie would be the only one trying to get a hold of her, and she'd see her in the morning. Her eyelids too heavy to deal with whatever drama she wanted to talk about, she closed her laptop and tossed it beside her on the couch. She flipped the television on to some mindless reality show. She was asleep before the first commercial break.

• • • • • • •

"Kara!" Her eyelids snapped open at the sound of her name being barked. Close, so close to her ear. The glow of the television played behind a silhouette of a figure, right in front of her. A heavy hand closed firmly against her mouth, muffling her cry of surprise. Hot breath scraped against her cheek. "Don't make a sound."

She tried to see him, this man squashing her lips against her teeth, but the TV illuminated the room behind him, casting him in darkness. She could only make out the largeness of his shoulders, and feel the weight of his strength as he continued to press his hand over her mouth.

He shifted on the couch, his knees coming to rest on the cushions on either side of her legs, pressing her harder into the pillow she had been sleeping on. Her mind unclouded, and she began to struggle against him. No way he was going to fucking rape her, or hurt her without at least feeling the bite of her nails across his skin. She clawed at him, his face, the hand trapping her air intake. Nothing fazed him.

He laughed. A low chuckle that at any other time she may have found sexy. Any other time she wasn't being pinned down to her couch with some stranger trying to rape her. Or worse.

"Fight all you want, kitty cat, but you won't get away. Now. I'm going to take my hand off your mouth, and we are going to talk. If you scream, yell, try to squirm away, there will be consequences. Do you understand? If you don't do what I tell you, there will be consequences."

The TV screen flashed white, casting some light across his features. Dark eyes stared down at her. Sharp-lined jaw clenched. She stopped struggling. The man was immovable, at least from her angle. He seemed to want an answer so she nodded, fully intending on scratching his eyes out once he released her.

He laughed again. "I don't believe you. But we'll see how this plays out." Slowly, as though finger by finger, he peeled his hand off of her mouth and sat back. She could feel his weight settling on her pelvic bones.

"Help!" she screamed and doubled her effort to get her nails into his face.

She heard the sigh, a heavy almost disappointed sound, just before his palm connected with her cheek. The sting of the slap shocked the words out of her. She'd received worse in a fist fight when she was a kid, but with him the meaning was crystal clear.

"I told you. You said you understood, which means either you're a liar or you aren't very smart. And I don't for a second doubt your intelligence." His lips brushed against her cheek as he spoke. She kept her face turned away from him, her hands pushing against his chest. His hard, broad chest that might as well have been made out of steel for all the success she had in shoving him off of her.

His hand snaked into her hair, gripping it at her scalp. She yelped when he shot off the couch and dragged her to her feet. Trying to slap his hands away from her head worked as much as shoving at him had, but she didn't stop from trying. "Now. We are going to have that talk, but if you make one more fucking move that I don't give permission for, I'm going to tie your little ass to a chair."

"No. Please." She tried to shake her head, but he held her steady.

"Ah, you do have manners. Good. You'll need them." He shoved her back onto the couch and let her go. While he walked to the other side of the room to flip the light switch, she eyed the front door. She might make it to the door before he turned around. It would be worth trying. He found the switch too easily. Hidden behind a bookcase, no one would know it was there if they hadn't been in her apartment before. She missed her chance, and he turned back to her, grabbing the chair from her desk and rolling it to the coffee table.

He sat across from her. The flimsy Ikea table was the only protection she had from him. With the lights on, she was able to see his features with more clarity. Chiseled nose, slightly off center as though it had been broken too many times to set correctly anymore. The sharp lines of his jaw and his cheekbones gave him a serious look, but his eyes. Dark brown eyes bore into her with an intensity that sent a shiver down her spine. The rest of him looked as large as she'd felt, but she could now see the dark tattoos running down both forearms. She didn't have time to see what they were of before he started talking.

"You have something that doesn't really belong to you." He leaned forward in the chair, resting his elbows on his knees.

She swallowed. "What are you talking about? I don't have anything."

"You do. Or at least you will, or should. I'm not really sure. That's why we're talking."

His features were familiar. "Devin?" She found his eyes, and even though her body begged her to look away, to find reprieve in staring somewhere else, she focused on the tiny wrinkles around his eyes as he smiled at her. It wasn't a warm smile. Not one that would send any fuzzy bunnies scampering toward him, but a steeled forced grin that made the danger in the room even more obvious.

He ignored her question. "You were at your brother's place a few days ago. Went in for a while and came out. You weren't in there cleaning up, but you didn't leave with anything in your hands either. What did you take?"

Her brother? Of course this had to do with Tommy. She had gone to his apartment a few days before, with no idea what she was looking for, but knew she had to look. When she'd gotten there the place had been ripped apart already. She hadn't cleaned any of it up.

She sat on the couch and stared at the place, willing her heart to stop hammering away in her chest. Her brother had gotten himself so deep into something, dying wasn't enough to get clear of it. Someone was looking for something. Hell, wasn't she? Answers maybe. Why'd they kill him, and why torture him first, why do the horrible things they did to him?

"Kara. The way this works is I ask you something, you answer."

Did he have a gun? Maybe she could get out of the apartment and away from him if he didn't have a gun. Since he hadn't shown it or pointed it at her, maybe he didn't.

"I'm gonna ask once more. What did you take from your brother's place?"

"Nothing." She pressed her palms together and tucked them between her knees. "It was all messy, someone else had been there. I just left." His dresser drawers had all been hanging out of the dresser, clothes thrown everywhere.

Couch cushions flipped, and papers strewn about.

"You were in there for a while, what were you doing?" The man didn't even blink.

"I missed him." Partially true. She did miss him, horribly. "I just—just wanted to be there." Still true. Even with him gone, being in his place, feeling his presence made the horror of losing him a little easier to bear.

He sat silently for a moment, but never looked away. His jaw clenched again. "Your brother left you something, isn't that right? And you're trying to find it." Another truth, but again partial.

"No, he didn't give me anything." Her eyes flickered to her laptop, only briefly, but he'd seen it.

"What's this?" He reached across the table and picked up the laptop. "Let's just see what you've been up to. Watching dirty movies?" She looked away then as the heat crept up her neck. When she peeked back at him, she was met with a raised eyebrow and a half grin, more playful than cynical. She should have wiped her history.

"What?" she barked at him, finding some bravery buried in her chest. The way he was looking at her, as though he had just seen something in her that he found interesting or amusing, sparked anger.

"We'll see." He gave her a slow wink and started tapping away on her computer. "Eagle, Michigan. Now why would you need to go there?" He reached behind him and every muscle in her body tensed, only to relax a fraction when he pulled out a cell phone. "Kara? I asked a question. What are you supposed to do when I ask you a question?"

"Go fuck yourself," she shot at him and crossed her arms over her chest. It wasn't wise; there wasn't a doubt in her mind this man would kill her just if the mood struck him, but she wouldn't show fear. Tommy had at least instilled that much into her. People like him fed off of fear. Well, he could just starve.

"And there went the manners." He let out a sigh again. She ignored the comment. She heard the laptop being placed on the table, heard him shuffle around with his cell, but still found herself surprised when he stepped over the table and grabbed her up by her arms. "It looks like we have a little trip to take." He dragged her away from the couch, ignoring her squirming as though she were just some errant bug that buzzed around him.

She realized where he was taking her, and her fight intensified. Her foot finally connected with his knee and he stumbled in his step. When he turned to look down at her, it was with a heated gaze that should have sent her shivering in fear, but it didn't.

With almost no effort, he spun her around and pushed her against the wall. A large hand held her firmly as the other hand slapped her ass four times. Hard, rapid slaps in the same spot on her left ass cheek, both surprising her and sending a burn through her body.

Spinning her back around to face him, he put his face in hers, leaving no room between their noses. "You do something like that again, and you'll get more than that. Got me?"

"You spanked me," she said with more surprise than hurt.

"That was a warning. Keep up this fighting me, and you'll see what a real spanking is." The warning came out in a low growl that suggested she probably didn't want to find out what he considered a real spanking to be. He finished dragging her into her bedroom and flung her on the bed. She bounced on the mattress and watched him, this stranger, go through her drawers until he found a pair of jeans. "Put these on." He tossed them at her then went in search of a shirt.

"You've been here before." She slid from the bed as she made that observation. He moved around the room as though he'd been there too many times before. He knew which drawer she kept her bras in.

"I do my homework." He tossed a bra at her then a t-shirt.

"This shirt doesn't fit." She held it out to him. The conversation felt insane. The whole fucking situation was insane. The man had broken into her apartment, threatened to hurt her, and obviously wasn't done with her if he was plucking out clothes for her. Yet, there she stood, holding out a shirt and asking for one that fit better. Her insides shook, and she wanted to ball up and cry, but she wouldn't. No fucking way she would show him how much his presence scared her. He wouldn't get that power. To make her feel something, to make her behave any other way than she chose.

"Put it on." He went to her closet and pulled down a small bag. She started to walk from the room but his hand shot out and grabbed her. "No. Here. You change here."

His eyes darkened again; that damn jaw looked as though it might break if he clenched it any harder. She gave a little nod and pulled away from him. As it was, she was sure to have a few bruises from their brief encounter. She turned away from him, facing the wall as she quickly shucked off her pajamas and shoved her legs and arms into the jeans and shirt. Like she said, it didn't fit. It had been a rash purchase, something cute she'd seen on the way to the register and had grabbed a size too small. Her breasts pushed through the fabric, straining the cotton trying to cover them.

While he was busy in the closet, she went into another drawer and pulled out a sweater, throwing it over her shirt. No need to tempt the madman.

Once he had what he wanted, he grabbed her arm again. "Let's go."

"I'm not going anywhere with you." She dug in her heels and fought him again. Nothing in their short history told her she would win, yet she continued to struggle.

He huffed and flung her ahead of him, then moved behind her. His arms slid beneath hers, and he gripped his wrists around her middle, pulling her tight against his chest. She was trapped. "You are coming with me." He grabbed her purse from the counter in the kitchen and held it in front of her, still keeping her neatly ensnared in his arms. "Your neighbor upstairs is on vacation, a little Hawaii getaway, and the apartment above him has been empty for two months." He had done his homework. "There's no one to help you. No one to hear you, but if you scream it will piss me off more than you already have. So, I wouldn't suggest you keep pushing it."

"I'm not going with you. If you want to kill me, you do it here." She tried to twist her torso one way then the other, but his arms were locked around her. She wasn't going anywhere.

"Oh, baby, that's not even on my radar. We have a lot of things to do, you and I, but killing you isn't one of them."

If he wasn't going to kill her, what the hell did he want her for? Her struggles amplified but he tamped them down with a bite to her neck.

"Keep that up, and you'll be sitting on a real sore ass."

Holding her around her middle, he frog-marched her from her apartment and up the five steps to the main entrance. She pushed back against him, trying to stall. Praying someone would be looking out of their windows, or walking down the street. But the street was black, the sun nowhere to be seen, and the moon hidden behind clouds.

As he shoved her toward a truck sitting in front of the building, a sickening realization hit her. No one was coming to help her. No one would witness her kidnapping. No one would find her.

CHAPTER THREE

Kara was no wilted flower. She struggled with him every step to the truck, not much of one given his years of training in the military, but she didn't give an inch. He managed to strong-arm her into the truck and behind the wheel, but she wasn't done fighting.

At full speed, she tried to throw open her door and jump out.

"What the fuck are you doing?" He managed to stop her by reaching his arm across the cabin and yanking her back by her hair—the only bit of her he could grab without driving them into a light post.

A pained yelp filled the small space and the door remained closed. Gripping her harder, and more pissed off than when he first wrangled her to the truck, he pulled her across the seat closer to him and pushed her head into his lap.

Between the pressure he had laid on her head, along with the pull of her hair, the woman should have been properly subdued. Instead, she flailed her arms until she found the steering wheel and tried to yank it from him.

Slamming on the brakes, he brought the truck to an immediate stop. His hand still entangled in her soft curls, he yanked her from his lap and brought her face close to his. "You have once choice to make now. It's the only decision I'm going to allow you from now on so make the right one. You either sit here like a good little girl or you can be gagged, tied, and thrown in the bed of the truck." The cover would at least keep her ass *in* the truck and would keep her from trying to kill him while he drove. "Do as you're told, or be punished. That's the only decision you get to make."

Her dark eyes widened, and those thick lips of hers pinched together. She didn't know what to do; both choices sucked for her. One meant she needed to submit to him, even if only slightly; the second left her bound and uncomfortable, not being able to see where they were headed or what was going on around her. After watching her over the past few weeks, he already knew she wasn't one to be kept in the dark. She needed to see everything, to know what was coming her way.

Devin gripped her hair harder. "Choose or I will, and like I said this is the only decision you get to make from here on out." Her jaw moved slightly, and he couldn't help the grin tugging at his lips. The girl had fire in her all right. "If you spit at me, I choose the truck bed after I punish you." He purposely lowered his voice, making her have to focus on his words.

She let out a long breath through her nose before she swallowed. He almost praised her for her self-control, but stopped himself. "I'll stay here." The words released on a whisper, but a steel thread had been laced in them.

One by one, his fingers let go of her hair, almost disappointed in the loss of contact with her. "Sit there. Keep quiet and do what I say. You do that, and you'll be fine. You keep up this attitude, this fight with me, you'll learn real quick you won't win." Her eyes had narrowed, but she didn't respond. She just scooted herself as far from him as she could, which was still completely within arm's length of him, and looked out the window.

He waited a minute before starting to move again. It was

still early; no cars were around to see them sitting there in the middle of the road. She didn't look back over at him. He watched her closely, expected her to start crying. She'd been kidnapped after all, and threatened. But there was nothing.

Devin turned his truck onto the I94 and gunned the gas, pushing them down the expressway. There was no real rush; he could take as long as he wanted now that he knew where he was going, and he had the hellcat somewhat subdued next to him. The speed reinforced to Kara, who was curled up in the seat beside him—in anger or fear, he wasn't quite sure—that she wasn't in control. It wasn't just the truck that he was driving, it was her future. He held it in his hands, and she needed to come to terms with that really quick if he was going to be able to get through the next few days with her still breathing.

Ten years in the military that included several deployments should have made him harder than this. He continued to check on her through the corner of his eye waiting for something. A tear, a sob, a sniffle. But nothing ever came.

The sun started rising. They'd made it out of Illinois in record time and were already half way through Indiana before she finally said something. He didn't understand what she said though. "What?" He looked over at her.

She tucked a curl behind her ear and faced him with steady resolve. "I need a washroom." She folded her arms over her chest. They'd only been on the road a few hours; he didn't want to stop yet. They had another five hours to go before they got to where they were going.

"We'll stop soon," he said and returned his gaze to the road.

"Stop now or you'll have to stop to clean the truck anyway." The words sounded more like a threat than an actual concern.

The next rest stop was coming up in two miles. There'd probably be people there, night travelers, early commuters; it would be a risk. "If I stop, you do exactly as I say. One little variation, one little mistake, and you'll regret it."

"Whatever. I just need to pee." She forced the carefree tone into her voice, but he didn't comment on it. Nor did he trust her.

He switched over to the right lane when the exit came up, and pulled them into the empty parking lot right in front of the brick building. They would have a bathroom and a few vending machines. Her shoulders slumped when she looked around the lot and took note of the abandoned area.

Turning off the truck, he pocketed the keys. "Stay right there," he ordered and jumped out, rounded the truck, and pulled her door open. "You stay right by me, and don't do anything fucking stupid in the bathroom like write on the mirror or the stall doors. I'm gonna check when you're done, so I wouldn't fucking do it—got it?"

"Or you'll punish me," she nodded and gave him a mocking grin. Oh, the girl had no idea what she would be getting herself into if she didn't start toeing the line. He gripped her upper arm, the sweater keeping him from touching what he imagined to be smooth skin that would be soft beneath his callused hands.

"You won't be grinning so much afterwards if I have to give you one. I promise you that." He brought his face closer to her, daring her to pull away, to yank her arm out of his hand, but she remained steady.

"Whatever." She rolled her eyes, but he had already seen her swallow back her fear. Good. It was about time she started to realize the danger she was really in.

He held onto her arm when she jumped from the cab of the truck, but slid his hand down to hers, entwining the fingers once they walked toward the building. Just a couple making a pit stop. Nothing to see here.

"Here." He pulled the rusted restroom door open and flipped on the light. A single room. Perfect. No window. Even better. "Go." He propelled her into the room and shut the door. He heard the lock slip in place as he leaned against it. It didn't matter. Other than living in there the rest of her life, there wasn't much else she could do.

Just as he heard the dryer turn on in the bathroom, the door to the building opened and an overweight, overtired truck driver shuffled in and headed to the second bathroom. Devin nodded in greeting, but otherwise ignored the man. The lock behind him slid open again and the door swung inward. Devin caught himself before he stumbled, but kept his eyes on the door of the second washroom.

He found her hand, gripped it even tighter, and tugged her forward. She pointed to the vending machines. "I'm hungry."

"We'll stop soon." Giving another look over his shoulder to make sure the trucker stayed inside the bathroom, he led them out of the annexed building and toward his truck.

Opening the passenger side door, he waved for her to get in. Once she was seated he put his hand on her thigh, squeezing the soft flesh to get her full attention. She covered his hand with her own, but didn't fight him otherwise. "So far so good." He flashed her a quick smile, gave her thigh a squeeze, and released her. He almost laughed at the narrowing of her eyes when he shut the door, but managed to keep a straight face. The girl had spunk, and she would need it to get through the trip. He wouldn't kill that fire in her; tamp it a bit, but never extinguish it.

As they pulled out of the lot and headed down the ramp toward the highway, her head snapped around to look out the window. Devin glanced in the rearview mirror and saw the truck driver walking out of the building and toward his truck.

"Dammit," he heard her mutter under her breath as she threw herself back around to face the front.

"You would have been stupid to try anything with that guy anyway," Devin remarked in a cool tone. The tension in her body was soaking up the air in the cabin of his truck. He knew she was terrified, and a healthy amount of fear was warranted, but terror made people panic. Panicked people did stupid things.

"You're right," she snapped. "Stick to the murderer you know, I always say, it's the unknown ones that'll really kill you." For a woman so afraid of being killed, she didn't harness her tongue very well.

"I've already told you, killing you isn't on the menu." He gripped the steering wheel harder, trying to keep the tension in his fingers and out of his voice.

She snorted. "I'm sure you told Tommy the same thing."

He looked over at her then, just in time to see her swipe a lone tear from her cheek and cock her head to the side. She was hurting, and nothing he said would really fix that, but he could give her the truth.

"I worked with Tommy, and we worked with some really fucked-up people. People you don't want to mess with, but I never did anything to Tommy. It wasn't me that killed him." He watched the road as he gave her as much truth as he could spare. She had no real reason to believe him. "I swear it to you, Kara. I did not kill your brother. I wasn't there and I had nothing to do with it." If he could have saved Tommy himself he would have in a heartbeat.

He chanced a glance over at her. Her eyes shimmering with unshed tears, she stared at him, indecision playing in her expression. "You know who did."

"I have a damn good idea, yeah."

"And those same people sent you for me."

He took a deep breath. "Yeah." When he looked back at her, she was staring at him. Her lips were parted and her eyes narrowed, but she remained silent. After a few quiet moments passed, she nodded and faced the road ahead again. The tension eased in her body, she actually rested her head against the headrest and closed her eyes. She believed him. She wasn't going to be offering him any sort of BFF badge, but at least she understood that he wasn't as horrible as she'd first imagined.

For the moment it would have to do.

• • • • • • •

As the sun made its way into the sky, the scenery outside the truck window became more vivid. Fall was approaching and many of the trees had already begun to twist away from their vibrant green to warm oranges and reds. It was her favorite season, yet as she watched the colors fly by the truck, she couldn't bring herself to feel anything other than the suffocating fear of what was coming her way.

Tommy never went into detail about his work, and kept her sheltered from the majority of his friends, but she'd seen a few before she moved out of Tommy's apartment. Once in a while they'd come pick him up at the apartment before she got in bed. Pleasant enough, they smiled, said hello, but once they thought she was out of hearing, she picked up on the tense tones, the cursing, the coded conversations. She didn't understand what they were all talking about, but she understood one thing. They weren't nice men, and Devin was one of them.

Devin hadn't shown her any weapon, but that didn't make her fear any less real. He probably didn't need a gun or a knife; those large hands of his could easily squeeze the life from her if he wrapped them around her throat. He'd told her he hadn't been the one to kill Tommy. It wasn't just the words; it was the way he told her. Like he needed her to believe him, not because he was tricking her. The other men Tommy hung around with had given her tingles in her spine; something was off with them. Devin didn't set off that alarm bell. She believed him; he wasn't going to kill her and he didn't kill Tommy. But that didn't make him safe either.

She needed to get away from him, before they got to wherever he was taking them. Assuming he had them pointed in the direction of Tommy's post office box, it would take several more hours to get there. Now that they were away from other people who could get hurt, she could plan her escape.

Devin reached over to the radio, flipping it on. Country

music filled the cabin, and she looked out the window. Would he turn it off if he knew she liked it? Just something else to use against her?

"You hungry?" His deep voice intruded on her brainstorming.

She didn't answer him. Instead she turned the knob and turned the sound louder.

"You worked with Tommy," she said, not looking at him. Tommy hated country music, and teased her incessantly when she was younger. *How can a girl living in Chicago love that farmer crap?* Yet, he'd let her put it on the radio every time he drove her in his car.

He glanced her way, then back at the road. "I think we covered that already."

"I saw you. I mean once. I was leaving and you were coming." She still couldn't bring herself to look at him. The tension rolling off his body filled the space between them.

"I remember," he nodded.

She did look at him then. "You do?"

He grinned, a sort of half grin, as though remembering something fondly. "Yeah, Tommy was trying to get you gone, but wanted you to take something. You wouldn't. When you walked past me you had your hands straight up in the air." He laughed, just a little. "Like a little kid, you looked. What was it anyway?" He moved in his seat, getting more comfortable.

"Money." She breathed out her answer and looked back out the window. If she'd taken it that day, or any other day he'd tried shoving an envelope of bills at her, she wouldn't have needed to even think about chasing down his post office box.

"You know what happened to him? You—" His jaw tensed and his grip tightened on the steering wheel.

"That's not going to happen to you." It was a vow.

"Because you're going to help me." She turned toward him, irritation starting to build up in her chest.

"I'm trying. Where were you going up this way? What's

in Eagle?"

She rolled her eyes and went back to trying to ignore him. Devin worked with the same shit Tommy did; the only person he was trying to help was himself. "I wasn't going anywhere."

He left it at that, letting a few songs play before he tried to speak with her again.

"You haven't eaten yet, it's near noon." Could that be actual concern from her kidnapper? Well, screw him.

She felt her stomach rumble at the mention of food, but thankfully it had been too quiet for him to hear. Or his manners kicked in and kept him from mentioning it.

"Open the glove compartment. There's a few bags of peanuts in there." He gestured toward the closed compartment. She didn't respond but didn't move either. "Get me the peanuts," he said with a harsher tone. One that suggested she do what he bid, but again… screw him. "Kara." Her name was given with exasperation. Tommy often made the same sound after going a few rounds with her in an argument. He wanted her to give in, do what he said. But she wasn't a giving in type of girl.

"Devin." She mimicked his tone. "I'm not hungry, and I don't give a shit if you are." She hadn't been prepared for him to react so quickly. The truck pulled to the side of the road. They'd already passed most of the touristy towns along the lake, making the road nearly deserted. He spun to face her and gripped her arm.

"Open the fucking compartment, Kara." His jaw tightened as he spoke.

Her insides shook with his intense stare, but she couldn't give in. She couldn't let him see how nervous she felt at that moment. The truck was stopped. A thick line of trees came into view. No more plotting or brainstorming; it was time to act.

Keeping her eyes fixated on his glare, she reached behind her and pulled the lever on the door, popping it open. She fell backward, half jumping, half falling to the ground. She heard his curse as her feet settled on the ground, and heard her name being bellowed as she took off running toward the trees.

Her feet hurt as she stepped on rocks and broken-off branches; the soft-soled tennis shoes she wore offered very little protection from such elements. Devin yelled again behind her. Closer now. She pushed harder. Each breath burned as she headed for the forest, only a few hundred more yards. How close was he behind her? She wanted to look, to turn her head, but forced herself to concentrate on the trees. Once she was in the woods she could zigzag and hopefully lose him among the dense forestry.

One bad step and her ankle rolled. She cried out from the pain shooting up her leg, but she pushed on. Kept running even though she limped. He wasn't calling her name anymore. Did that mean she'd outrun him?

The trees were around her suddenly; she was inside the woods. Running to the right, she watched the wooded carpet, watching for roots or limbs that would trip her up again. Her ankle screamed with each step, but she kept going.

A clearing came into view. She needed to make a decision: run for the clearing and hope there was a house nearby, or keep to the thick woods.

Either way was taking a chance.

She cut to the right, her foot grazing over a fallen tree just as a heavy hand wrapped around her arm, yanking her back. The log broke her fall, and his full weight came down over her body, crushing her into the leaves on the ground.

"You ran." The heat of his breath warmed her already sweaty face.

Kara kicked her legs up, but no good came of it. He adjusted his weight so that her legs were completely immobilized, as was the rest of her. Arms pinned beneath her, face squished into the dirty ground. Everything hurt and burned, and she wanted to breathe. So badly she wanted to breathe again.

Why wasn't he saying something? She could only hear him panting over her. He began to move over her, twisting from one side to the other. Her lungs expanded and she took a deep breath. She heard a jangling of metal, and the sound of leather being pulled through fabric. She'd heard that sound before. Had come to crave it. Now that she heard it firsthand, she began to struggle with everything inside of her. She didn't know him, didn't know what he was capable of, but whatever was coming her way she wanted no part in it.

His knee sank into her back, and she cried out. Completely immobilized beneath his firm hold, she could only listen and feel as he shifted again, lifting off of her body, except for that damn knee pinning her to the ground.

"I'm trying to help you, Kara. But you just won't listen." His knee shifted on her back, but he didn't get off of her. "You've always wondered, always craved it, but you've never had it. Well, now's as good a time as ever."

Fingers dove into her hair, pulling her head back until she could see upward. His face appeared before her. Dark, stern eyes and firm jaw. "You didn't listen. You were a bad girl, Kara. And you know what happens to bad girls." She only had a moment to be confused by his words.

A sharp, hot pain slashed across her ass. Then again. Her throat burned anew, this time from her screaming. Her hands clawed at the ground, trying to get free of his punishing hand, his heavy knee. No relief came. Nothing she did moved him. Again and again the fire spread across her ass. Tears welled up in her eyes, slipping free without thought of stopping them.

"Stop!" she screamed and bucked, but he didn't seem interested in listening.

"I warned you, Kara. I told you I'd punish you if you didn't listen." How could he be so calm? So in control while taking a belt to her backside? Because he was a madman.

"Okay! Okay!" She wiggled harder, but still he was unmoved. "Okay!" Finally, the pain in her ass rocketed her out of herself. He wouldn't stop until she was subdued, until she gave in to him. Her body responded before her mind, and went limp beneath him. The struggling stopped, the wiggling and fighting no longer an option. She'd lost.

The leaves lying on the ground in front of her moved with her heavy breathing. Dirt ground into her forehead, but she didn't care. Her ass hurt, felt swollen and raw. The spanking had stopped, his belt slid back into his jeans, but his knee remained in place.

"We're going to get up and go back to the truck." His hand went back into her hair, fisting her hair at the scalp, and pulled her to her knees then to her feet.

Tears rolled down her face, hot and sticky, but she made no move to wipe them off. In the end she didn't need to. She was turned to face him and his free hand wiped the fat drops of water away with the back of his hand.

"You've lost the privilege of sitting in the truck with me." His eyes weren't dark anymore, and his jaw no longer clenched in anger. He almost looked handsome with his hair disheveled from their struggle, his chest still heaving a bit from the run.

"What do you want?" she whispered into the small space between them.

He frowned. "Your obedience, Kara."

What do you say to a crazy person? Her obedience? She would never obey him, never surrender.

"I'm trying to help you, but I can't do that if you won't listen to me." He was worse than crazy, he was delusional.

Instead of telling him how nuts she believed him to be, she tried to pull herself from his grasp. He proved too strong once more and sighed. Another hint of disappointment laced in the heavy sound. "Whatever Tommy was messed up with, I had no part of it. I don't want any part of it." She ground her teeth together. The more she tried to help her brother over the years, the more dangerous his world became.

Devin's frown intensified. "It's a bit late for that, I

think."

"Whatever he left, whatever you're looking for. Just take it. Take it." Fuck the money. She'd just keep working, she'd get her savings account filled again. She didn't need Tommy's dirty money—she never should have tried for the easy way. Tommy had always gone the easy route, and look how it ended for him.

"And you'll just turn the other cheek? Won't breathe a word of the last twelve hours to anyone?" His grip softened in her hair, but not enough to twist away from him.

"Right. That's right. I won't say a word. Not about you breaking in, or… or… what you just did." Her lips dried at her quick breathing.

The edges of his mouth curled up, a deep crevice outlined his grin. "What did I just do?" Was he taunting her? Laughing at her?

"You know what you did." Her ass still throbbed from the lashing.

"Tell me." He whispered his command, but it held all the authority of any other demand he'd made. "The fantasy of a spanking is a hell of a lot better than the reality, isn't it? At least when you're getting it for being a naughty girl."

"I hate you." She closed her eyes and when she opened them, his frown was back.

"It's probably best you do. Now do what I said. Tell me what I did."

"Fuck you." She tried to pull away, but as was rapidly becoming customary, her struggles had no impact.

"Maybe at our next stop. Not now though. You haven't earned it." His words struck her and her eyes flew open, searching his face. The damn grin was back. "Think I didn't notice how dilated your eyes are? I can only imagine how wet your pussy is right now. If the truck wasn't sitting on the highway over there, I'd dip my finger in to find out, but as it is, and like I said, you haven't earned it yet." He gave her a tug. "Now tell me what I did back there, what you did earn from me."

As much as she wanted to swing her leg back and plant her foot in his balls, the fire still burned bright in her ass and set her mind straight. She huffed, determined to outwait him, but the man looked as though he had all day.

"You." She sighed again, her stomach fluttering as the words tumbled through her mind. Experiencing it hadn't been hard enough, now she had to vocalize it. His gaze only burned hotter the longer she stalled. "You hit me."

"Try again."

His patience waned as his jaw clenched tighter.

She knew what he wanted, knew he hadn't hit her, not really. He had warned her, had promised she'd get more of what he gave her in the hallway of her apartment if she kept it up. But that didn't mean she was going to go along with it.

One dark eyebrow raised and arched. He wasn't going to wait forever.

"You spanked me," she croaked. The fire in her cheeks completely mirrored that in her ass with her admission.

"The fantasy isn't so great in real life?" He released her hair and his hand ran over the spot he'd been yanking. He'd said the same thing just before he started laying into her with his belt. He'd seen her computer, but not for long; he couldn't have seen her hidden history.

"Come on." He nudged her toward the truck.

She wouldn't let him drag her, not this time. Kara kept up with his long stride by half jogging beside him to the truck. Once they were at the truck, she tried to move toward the passenger side door. He shook his head and pulled her to the back of the truck.

No cars drove past on the highway. Not one damn soul would be helping her.

"Nope. I told you. You lost that privilege." He turned the handle of the trunk and lowered the door. The cover over the bed made it look ominous and dark. And hot. With one hand on her, he used his free hand to pull out a small tackle box.

He pulled out a small ball gag and several zip ties. Not items one would typically see in a tackle box, but she wasn't exactly in the position to shoot off her mouth. "No, please. Don't." She tried to turn her head when he came at her with the ball gag.

"I warned you, and I don't go back on my promises. If I tell you you'll be punished, then you'll be punished. Learn this lesson now and avoid it in the future." His words made it clear he planned on her spending more time with him than just a quick run up to a post office box. If all he wanted was the contents of that box, they wouldn't need to be together for more than half a day.

He shoved the silicone ball between her teeth. Kara tried to bend forward, to ram into his stomach, but he held her hard. She ran on pure adrenaline, needing to get her hands away from him before he got those ties around them. Devin might as well have been a semi-truck, for all the good her struggles did. He had her wrists behind her and zipped up in the plastic binds before she could so much as maneuver her footing to break free. The buckle of the ball gag pinched a piece of her hair, and her wrists hurt when she tried to pull free.

"Struggling will only hurt you. Now up." He scooped her off the ground and slid her into the bed of the truck. When her feet were the only part of herself still outside, she felt more ties slip around her ankles. She kicked out, tried to pull her legs apart, but he corralled them with the skill no man should possess. "There you go. All tucked in nice. Now. Lie here like a good girl. We'll be there in a just a few short hours. If you can behave, maybe I'll take the gag out when we get there." The bed of the truck was dark, the only light coming from where he was crouched down looking at her from the open door. He gave her a slow wink and shut it, taking all the light away.

She tried to wiggle, to kick, to scream but it didn't matter. She was effectively trapped. The truck roared to life, sending vibrations throughout the bed.

Kara closed her eyes as she felt the truck move out onto the road again. So much for her escape. She was more stuck than before.

CHAPTER FOUR

The truck rolled over the smooth pavement of the highway with little noise. Either Kara had fallen asleep or given into her fate, because she wasn't making a sound back there. The first hour had been full of banging and muffled yelling; both were covered up nicely with a quick turn of the volume. After that he focused on what was coming up for them.

He promised himself when he took the job to finish it quickly, cleanly then get the fuck out. Get moving onto the next phase in his life, free of criminal assholes who took life for granted, and those who would hunt them down at any cost.

Except things weren't going as planned. Drive from point A to Point B in a straight line. That was his plan, that was the way to do things cleanly. Yet, there he was, pulling off the fucking highway and headed down to point C.

He would finish the job, he never left a mission incomplete, but first he needed information. Kara may or may not know things, but either way he needed to be sure. Sure that she was innocent, or positive that she was as dirty as her brother. In his world, siblings stuck together, more so when circumstances shoved them in shitty places.

Devin didn't go into a job without knowing the facts, covering all angles of what he might find. Her computer had been a fucking treasure trove, one that would be useful in the coming days if she didn't start cooperating a little better. Twisting someone's darkest desires for his own purpose may have made him a bastard, but the job would be done, and he'd be gone. Find the weakness, then go for the kill, his mom had told him. She may have been talking about football strategy, but the lesson still applied.

The sun sank lower in the sky, shooting off soft shades of orange across the evening sky. The building he'd been looking for finally came into view. The dirt of the road kicked up around the truck as he pushed the gas. A large farmhouse, long ago abandoned and just barely finished being remodeled greeted him, reminding him what he was working toward. His reward when all the bullshit settled.

Gravel crunched beneath the wheels of his Ford pickup. Throwing the truck into park, he leaned his head back against his seat and took a deep breath. Too many ideas running through his head, too many motives trying to be resolved.

A loud thump brought him back to reality. He could figure out the rest later; first he had to deal with his little escape artist. She had almost outrun him, if she hadn't scraped that log as she hurtled over it, she may have actually made it to the clearing. And after that, he didn't know what was behind there. Probably some hermit trying to stay under society's radar, and the last thing a hermit wanted was a crazed woman running up his yard yelling for help.

His door creaked when he closed it. Another thump and a muffled scream. As afraid as she obviously was, she did her best to keep her features from showing it. She sucked at it, but she was trying.

Devin slid the key into the trunk, twisting the handle slowly, and braced himself for her to try launching herself out of the bed when he opened it. She didn't make a move. Finally, she was using some sense.

"Time to come out of there." He reached his long arm in and found her foot, yanking on her leg to slide her toward the opening. Still no struggle. That should have been his warning.

Just as her feet cleared the bed, she bent her legs up and thrust them forward, striking him in the chest with both feet. The wind flew from his lungs as he landed on his ass.

She wiggled the rest of the way out and got to her feet. Her ankles were still bound, her hands were behind her, and her mouth was sopping wet with the drool from the ball gag. Brown curls stuck to her cheek where her spittle had dripped while she laid in the truck bed. He couldn't help the way his body reacted to the sight before him, but he tried to shove away the desires. She was his captive, not his toy.

"You'll pay for that one later." He got to his feet, while she looked around. Probably trying to find the best way out. "There's nowhere to go, and you'd have to hop the entire way." He slapped his hands across his jeans, brushing the dust from the material. "Even if you did manage it, it's about five miles before you get to a road, and another three before you hit a neighbor." Eight miles between him and any other living soul. It was perfect.

Kara shot him a glare, narrowed eyes and bright red cheeks, but didn't try to move. More than likely she'd fall on her face if she tried.

"Turn around." He circled his finger in the air. She shook her head. Even when she had no choice, nowhere to go, still she held onto her defiance. "I've lost my patience with you." He touched his belt buckle. "I want to take the damn ties off, if you can behave yourself."

Kara's eyes watched his hands and she quickly shuffled her feet until her back was to him, pushing her hands out toward him. He wasn't going to be that generous, but at least she listened to him. He pulled his pocket knife out of his boot and bent down to cut away the zip ties around her ankles. "If you kick me again, you'll regret it. I promise you. You already have to answer for that last one."

She muttered something but the words were lost in the gag.

She waved her hands at him again, which he grabbed with one of his own, pulling her back against him. His mouth pressed against her ear. He inhaled, taking in her scent. Even through the sweat, he could smell the sweetness of her bath gel. Peach. The woman spent over two hours cooped up in a hot trunk, and she smelled of peaches.

"Here's what's going to happen, peaches. We are going to go inside, and you are going to behave yourself. Sit where I tell you, and talk when I tell you. I'll take the gag off once we're inside. Nod your pretty little head if you understand me." He felt more than saw her movement, as his lips were still pressed up against her ear. He nipped her earlobe then pulled away. "Walk." He held onto her wrists and aimed her toward the front steps of the farmhouse.

Remodeling had just finished. Nothing had been moved in yet, but it was livable. For them at least. The finished project would be something else entirely. The little carrot at the end of the stick. And after this job was completed that damn carrot would be all his.

He dug out his key for the front door, keeping her facing away from him as he unlocked the door and pushed it open. "Inside." He pulled on her wrists to get her moving. She looked over her shoulder at him as she passed by, her eyes promising him revenge at the first chance she got. Unluckily for her, she wouldn't get that chance.

Once the door was closed, he flipped the lock and leaned against the door, letting her wander down the hall. Paint fumes still lingered from the last bit of construction, but overall everything looked perfect. The hardwood floors had exactly the old worn look he wanted, and all of the molding matched beautifully. A rustic old farmhouse where he would ride out his retirement the only way he knew how.

He followed behind her as she walked into the living room off the main foyer. A few folding chairs were scattered around and several TV trays were still left out from the construction crew's lunches probably. A large fireplace on the northern side took up most of the wall. He would need to get the interior decorator in soon to deal with rugs and artwork. To fill in whatever spaces were left after he hung his own pieces. He had no knack at décor; he knew what he liked and what he didn't, but putting them all together to make a room? Not for him.

"Sit in that chair." He pointed to one of the folding chairs. Without another look in his direction, she took a seat. "I'll take the gag out, but if you scream, spit, or cuss at me, it goes back in after you get your ass blistered. Understand, peaches?"

She eyed him with caution but slowly nodded her agreement. He doubted she could behave for longer than the conversation they were going to have, but he would deal with her if she didn't. The only way they were going to get through this mission was if she listened to him and learned to follow his lead and not reach for the reins.

Devin gripped the ends of the gag and began to unbuckle the leather straps. After it was all unbuckled he pulled it forward and popped it out of her mouth. She clamped her lips closed, working her jaw open and shut several times while trying to lick the spit from her chin.

His hands cupped her face then swiped over her cheeks, taking away the pools of her saliva. He could smear it further along her cheeks and nose, could humiliate her in that way, but the point here wasn't to humiliate her. He needed her cooperation and obedience. "There. Not so bad, right?" He gave her a wink and pulled up another chair to face her.

"You beat me." Her voice sounded gravelly, as though she'd been screaming in the truck. He hadn't heard her, and he would have if she had been loud enough.

"I spanked you," he corrected, folding his arms over his chest and settling into the metal chair. "There's a difference, and we already covered that."

"Whatever." She rolled her eyes and turned to look out the window. The plastic coverings allowed some light into the room, but with the sun so low in the sky it wasn't enough to see much.

"Now. I'm going to ask you some questions, and you'll answer them honestly. If you lie, or I think you're lying, there will be consequences. If you try to run, or hurt me in any way, there will be even bigger consequences. Understand, peaches?"

"My name is Kara," she shot at him, twisting in her chair to push her wrists through the opening in the back. A little comfort in an otherwise shitty situation.

He sighed. "Where were you headed when you got to Eagle?"

"Nowhere. I was just going on a little vacation," she shrugged, her eyes settled on space behind him.

"That's one lie. Now. I'll ask again. Where were you going? What were you going up there for? Your brother leave something for you?" It wasn't uncommon in the lifestyle Tommy led, and from what Michael had told him, there was definitely something needing to be found. Everything having to do with incriminating him. When you're the head of a crime family, incriminating evidence is something to be concerned about.

"I told you I had nothing to do with what Tommy got himself involved in. I wanted him out of that crap, whatever that crap was." She rubbed her chin against her shoulder. For a moment he imagined her years younger, trying to talk Tommy out of going to work. Her relentless glare wouldn't have been a match for her older brother, already set in his ways. Already starting to make a name for himself.

"You have no idea what your brother was doing? How he was getting money?"

She rolled her head to bring her eyes in line with his. Exhaustion played in her stare. "I told you I don't know anything, and I was just going to get away for a little while. So, you should just let me go."

He laughed. "Right. That's going to happen." He leaned forward, resting his elbows on his knees. "I'm going to ask you once more. This is your last chance, then I'm going to start giving you the rules and regulations of this place, and you won't like the rules if you don't behave."

She pushed her face forward, nearly brushing his nose with her own. "Fuck. You." A small part of him admired her for her stubbornness. The rest of him wanted to tamp down the bravado and get to her truth. Everyone had a truth buried inside, deep down.

"I think it's time for a tour." His hand snaked around her neck and gripped her hair in a fist.

• • • • • • • •

The man had a grip like a vise. She found herself being pulled to her feet and propelled forward.

When she stepped too far ahead, he pulled her back. They walked through what would be a living room into a larger room. Just as the first, a few chairs were scattered around, but no other furniture filled the space. Drywall had been put up recently; she could smell the spackle on the walls.

He didn't speak as he pushed her through the room and into a hallway. A narrow space between the stairs leading to the second floor. She recognized the kitchen because unlike the other rooms, it had some furniture. All the appliances were in place, and appeared new, as well as a table with several chairs surrounding it. But he didn't stop in the kitchen either.

"Through here." He tugged her hair when she tried to stop, tried to dig her heels in. A closed door at the far corner of the kitchen, tucked between a refrigerator and a pantry. He reached around her and turned the knob, yanking the door toward them.

Darkness hovered around her as she took her first steps down into the basement. She expected to smell mold and dust; however, the scent of fresh paint greeted her as they made their descent. "Careful, the last step is higher off the floor."

A soft light flickered to life over her head, lighting up the rest of the stairs. His grip softened enough for her step down each step without her hair being yanked from her head, but still he remained attached to her.

The last step was indeed higher than the rest, and she stumbled a bit before steadying her footing. "There's a switch… ah, here it is." He reached around her, brushing his body against hers as he flipped the lights on. A kidnapping bastard shouldn't smell so damn good. The scent of soap mingled with a musky aftershave. "Good. They said it was pretty much finished." He moved his hand from her hair to her upper arm and dragged her forward.

She yanked free of his hold and took in her surroundings. Freshly applied deep purple paint donned the walls, giving it a sinister appearance. The medieval-looking sconces on the walls used for lightening didn't lighten the mood at all, nor did the half dozen metal rings embedded into the walls and the two hanging from the ceiling. The hardwood floors had a nice polish to them, which accented the wooden furniture in the room. A large four-poster bed sat in the far corner of the room, as though to mock her with its innocent appearance. A leather armchair occupied the space beside the bed. In the other corner, away from the bed stood a cage. The cage was large enough for an adult to stand upright and walk a few paces in each direction.

She turned to him, surprised to find him staring at her.

"W-what is this place?" she asked, noting for the first time the rack behind him on the wall. Over a dozen hooks, each holding some instrument of discipline, covered the dark wood. Floggers, paddles, whips, and other devices she wasn't sure she'd seen before, not in any of her online journeys, not even in the darkest of her searches.

"This is the main house." His answer didn't really answer anything. "But this room, this is where naughty girls have their time-outs." He grabbed her arm again and headed for the cage. She yanked back, tried to free herself, tried to kick at him. She would not go into that fucking cage. Not quietly and not without protest.

"Let me go!" She kicked at him again, losing her balance and falling to her knees. He let her go momentarily, only to readjust his grip and help her back up to her feet.

"If you keep lying to me and being a bad girl, this is where you'll stay. But if you start behaving, being my good girl, then I'll let you stay upstairs with me. The master bedroom has been finished for some time; I'll even let you sleep in the bed, have a nice warm shower, and get some rest. But only if you start answering my questions with honesty."

His chiseled features gave nothing away, no emotion played through his dark eyes. He didn't seem to care which way it went, after all, he'd get what he wanted from her. She didn't think the man had a single doubt in his mind about that.

"I don't know what Tommy was into." She closed her eyes. Tommy made it a point to keep her in the dark. Protecting her was what he said, but she didn't care what he called it. She never wanted to know what he did, or how he got his money. She wanted him to stop, to get a real job with a real paycheck. Maybe something that didn't involve the gun he kept hidden in his nightstand.

"Tell me why you were headed to Michigan. What's up in that little dinky ass town?" He released her arm, but grabbed at the waist of her jeans when she tried to step away. "Tell me, peaches. Tell me where you were going." His voice dipped, low and sultry the same as his eyes that were now fully focused on her. His fingers played with the button on her jeans.

"You rape me, I kill you. That's how that's going to work," she spat at him.

He tensed. "I can understand your worry, but what you see isn't always what's in front of you. I don't rape women or kill them." His jaw clenched and released with his statement, as though the idea of going that far, doing something that repugnant turned his stomach. His eyebrow raised as he unbuttoned her jeans and slid one hand down the front, beneath her panties and lower still until he reached her pussy. One finger dipped lower, brushing over her clit. She caught the moan in her throat before it escaped. "See, you never learned to hide your emotions very well. Everything you think, you feel, crosses your face. You saw this room, the floggers, the paddles, and your eyes lit up like a little girl on Christmas morning."

He was lying. He had to be. She'd learned a long time ago to keep her desires to herself. As for hiding her emotions from her features, he probably had that pegged well enough. She'd never had to hide before, not general thoughts or feelings. It was the darker side of herself she kept locked up tight, and it was that part of herself he claimed to be seeing now in the makeshift dungeon she found herself standing in, arms bound.

A thick finger slid lower still, through her folds that were wet beyond her will, and toyed with the rim of her entrance. She fought back the moan burning her throat, and censured her body for moving, arching toward his touch.

"Stop." She tried to pull free, to move away from his touch, but his hand was as good as trapped in her jeans. "Don't." His finger only became more insistent, bending at the knuckle and sliding inside of her. Years had passed since the last time a man touched her in such a way.

"Fuck, you're tight." He pulled her closer to him, pressing her body against his. The hard length of his cock pressed through his jeans against her hip, and for a brief moment she hoped he'd replace his finger with it. What the hell was wrong with her? "And wet as hell," he muttered against her ear. His lips trailed her earlobe as he spoke.

His finger moved within her and the heel of his palm ground into her clit. Her body pulled away from her mind, reveling in the sensations. The pleasure of feeling full, and touched, and pleasured. "Please," she whispered, finally finding her sense. She couldn't like what he was doing. It was wrong.

"Please more? Please let you come?" Her clit swelled beneath the ministrations of his hand. The pressure increased against her clit, his finger picked up the pace, and his heated breath playing against her ear drove her closer to an edge she did not want, but needed all the same. "Tell me where you were headed, and I'll let you come. You'll come so hard, you'll forget what you were fighting against to begin with." More pressure, faster thrusts.

Her knees buckled. She leaned forward into his chest, using him to hold her upright. If he kept it up, she'd embarrass herself by coming all over his fingers. Could she do it quietly, maybe slip it past him? She'd get what she wanted, and he'd be left in the cold.

"Tell me, peaches, or this gets a lot less pleasurable." He nipped her earlobe, sending more electric currents down her body. Damn him. "For you anyway."

"I—" She took a deep breath, arched her hips toward him just a little more, just a few more seconds and she'd find her fulfillment. "I was going—" Almost. The pressure was damn near unbearable; it had to be released. "I was going to—" There. Right there the first signs of her orgasm revving up began and just as she was about to plummet into the valley of ecstasy, his hand yanked free of her jeans and he pushed her away from him, still holding her up by her arm.

A dark smile crossed his lips. "Now, now. No stealing. You'll get an orgasm when you've earned it, peaches. Everything you get from me will be earned. Even the basics, like clothes. That is, if you keep up this little game. If you'll just cooperate we can get down to business and move forward."

"And then you'll dump me off somewhere? Bring me back to Michael? He's the one that sent you, right? Tommy's big bossman?" The sobering thought kicked away her arousal; the painful bite of an orgasm denied still lingered, but she no longer teetered on that edge. She could just tell him what she was looking for, where Tommy had told her to go, let him deal with all of that and be done with it all.

"You don't know as much as you think you do, little girl." His eyes darkened, and his jaw firmed again. Had she offended him? Was it such a large leap to believe he'd abandon her? Of course he would; why would he waste his time on a nobody like her?

"If you knew who killed Tommy, why didn't you do something about it? Why didn't you try to stop it?" Kara's back stiffened. She had seen Tommy's body after the police turned it over to her for burial. Nightmares contained the images she witnessed when she saw him. "Why?" she yelled in his face. Her breath coming faster, the familiar clench of panic in her chest gripped her.

CHAPTER FIVE

Kara's eyes went wide, darting from him to the rest of the room. He'd seen the same look in combat; he'd smelled the same scent then too. Fear.

His hand wound tight into her scalp, holding her head still. As afraid as he knew she was, she held herself upright, clenched tight. Not wanting him to see her emotions, even when they played so openly across her features.

"Answer my question, Kara. What were you going to do once you got to Eagle?"

Her nostrils flared as she took deep breaths. He shouldn't have touched her earlier, shouldn't have put his fingers in her pussy, because all he wanted to do at that moment was finish the job. Her pupils were still dilated, and he could still smell her arousal on his fingers.

"The post office." Her teeth clenched together as she spoke.

"Why the post office?"

"Why did they kill Tommy?"

He yanked on her hair harder, enjoying the wince of pain she granted him. "Why the post office?"

"I hate you." She spat at him. A trickle of spit ran down his chin.

He didn't answer. Instead he released her hair and gripped the neckline of her sweater. With one strong yank, he tore the material and ripped it from her body. She tried to move away, out of his grasp, but he didn't pay attention to her movements. She would learn, she would begin to understand that the only hope she had of getting out of this alive was to trust him, to obey him.

Her chest heaved against the tightness of her t-shirt. He wanted to rip it all off, but he changed his mind just before reaching for her again. He whipped out his pocket knife and made quick work of cutting through the ties on her wrists, before spinning her back around to him. "Take off your clothes. All of them." To show her that he wasn't going to touch her, he crossed his arms over his chest. Her eyes darted toward the stairs. "I'll catch you, and it will be bad. Real bad for you if you run. Do what I say. Take off your clothes."

"And if I don't?" Her chin tilted up. So much defiance for such a little thing.

"If you don't, I'll take my belt to your ass again, and you'll do it anyway."

"Why can't you just let me go, leave me be?" He didn't like the desperation in her voice.

"I don't want to." He shrugged. "Now, strip." She couldn't see any shake in his resolve. A firm grip on the situation, that's what he needed. What she needed.

She stared at him with strong eyes and clenched jaw. Heavy breathing made her nostrils flare and her chest buck against that damn t-shirt. It was too tight for her breasts. She had told him that, but he hadn't given a shit. Not that he did at that moment either. The woman had nice tits, from what he could see from the outside. Fuck, he should control himself better. He had a job to do, a mission to complete.

A thick curl fell over her face. "I—why?" The fight came back to her voice. Even better.

"Because." Truths were earned, and at that moment she was working her way to a strong deficit. "Do it now. If I have to do it, I promise you'll be getting a belting." He purposely dragged his gaze over to the bench situated in the corner of the room. A spanking bench he'd had specially ordered for his private room in the farmhouse. The contraption was positional, which left so many options open either for punishments or for pleasure. "You lost the privilege of clothing when you spit on me." He would give her that much, but nothing more.

"Fu—" Before she could get the rest of her word out, he was on her. If she wouldn't listen, he'd have to show her, have to prove to her that his words were always to be taken as gospel. If he promised an ass whipping, she'd get one.

He yanked her toward the bed, forgoing the bench for another time. This would be quick, no need to mess with ties and cranks. She shrieked when he threw her over the side of the bed. Her feet didn't touch the floor in her position, her toes barely scraped it as she kicked and squirmed. Digging his knee into her back, he ripped his belt off. Doubling it over, he moved his own positioning to hold her down with one strong hand on her back, removing his knee to give himself a larger target. Her ass wiggled beneath him. The round globes would look so much better bare, bouncing from each lash of his leather, but this was a lesson, not a pleasure session.

"I warned you. I told you what would happen." The belt crashed down over both cheeks, and she bucked up.

"Stop! Please!" More than likely her ass was still sore from the first belting, but she obviously hadn't learned her lesson. A whipping and being tied up in the trunk bed had taught her nothing.

"Not until I'm done." Another lash, across the backs of her thighs. She howled at the tender spot of her legs being thrashed.

He continued bringing the belt down, watching her wiggle, enjoying the sounds of her pleading for him. He shouldn't. He shouldn't be spanking her, and he sure as fuck shouldn't have found so much damn enjoyment in it. But there it was anyway. His cock lengthened in his pants, hardening beyond discomfort. A just punishment for breaking his own rules.

"Please. I'm sorry I spit on you!" She reached back, grabbing at his arm. He avoided her hand, but barely, so he grabbed her hand and pinned down to keep from hitting anything other than her beautiful ass. "Just a bit more, and then you'll get up and do what I said. Understood?" He paused the strokes and waited for her answer.

Heavy breathing and a sniffle answered him. Another harsh stroke to the gentle curve of her cheeks, and he waited again. "Okay!" Another sniffle. "Fine. I'll do it." Her head flopped onto the mattress, her shoulders shook slightly.

Experience told him she'd had enough for that moment. Was he a complete bastard because he still wanted to give her a few more licks? To see how much she could take for him? Of course he was, and he wasn't about to play with that demon just yet, not without her being ready. And she was anything but ready for play. Devin moved off her and stood to the side. If she was waiting for him to help her up, she'd be sorely disappointed. She got herself in that position, she'd get her damn self out of it. She looked over her shoulder. Was she hoping he wouldn't be there, watching her move herself up to a standing position after being spanked? The humbling act would do her some good. He couldn't do his job if she kept holding back, kept trying to escape him. The sooner she got with the program, the sooner they could get done with it all. And he could walk away.

He was about give her another taste of the belt to get her to obey, when she finally started to move. Slow, deliberate movements as she pushed herself off the bed. Brown curls hid her expression from him as her fingers toyed with the hem of her shirt. In one swift movement, like ripping off a Band-Aid, she pulled the shirt over her head and dropped it on the bed. Her hands disappeared behind her back momentarily while she unfastened her bra—a feat even at the age of thirty-two Devin found fascinating. The cotton cups sagged over her breasts once the clasp was free and her hands moved back to her front, holding the cups there, still not looking up at him.

Part of him expected defiance in her gaze, for her to glare at him while she complied with his order. Instead she looked almost embarrassed. Had no other man seen her naked before? Surely she wasn't that innocent.

"Have you been naked with a man before?" The question fell out of his mouth, startling her. Her hands pressed against the cups of her bra harder, she looked at him through the curls hanging over her face.

"Yes." Her throat contracted, her jaw clenched a bit harder. He sensed she told the truth, but her actions suggested that she may have been naked with a man before, but not many. Maybe only one or two.

Being made to strip in front of a stranger probably slowed her movements, but it was her inexperience that made her look away from him, hiding her features behind those damn curls.

He let her take a moment, and almost smiled when she went back to her task. She relaxed her grip and slid the bra down her slender arms. She had some muscle in her biceps, enough for him to know she put effort into it.

Her breasts. Fuck, her tits were gorgeous. Not fake, though. No, the round, perfectly weighted breasts were all real. Her dark nipples hardened beneath his gaze, coming to peaks. Either from the slight chill in the room, or arousal. It didn't matter, although he suspected it to a mixture of both.

"Keep going, peaches." He tapped the belt against his thigh. She took the message and gingerly slid her gentle hands into the waist of her pants, and she pushed them over her hips. She grimaced a bit when the material scraped against her ass. He noticed, and so did his dick.

If she bothered to look up at him, she'd see his hard-on pressing against his jeans. She'd see how fucking turned on he was by her body, her obedience, and by the very idea of how red her ass had to be at that moment.

She scooped her panties down with the jeans. Efficient, and another way to avoid having to peel the last layer of clothing away from her body in front of him. He'd have to be more careful with his wording in the future, make sure she didn't have any loopholes to jump through again.

Her breasts swung as she bent over to pick up the jeans-panties bundle and toss them on the bed. He almost reached out and tweaked her nipples. Almost. At least he still had some self-control left.

Completely naked, save for her socks, she stood in front of him, arms folded over her stomach, her face turned away from him. He soaked up the sight before him. Muscular legs led up to a small patch of hair just above her pussy. Neatly trimmed and cropped short. Even in the dim lighting of the room he could make out the bit of moisture on her lips.

"Time for bed, little girl." He tossed his belt on the bed and gripped her upper arm. He needed space. If he kept looking at her like that he'd be too hard pressed to continue being a gentleman. She would probably laugh at his claiming to be one, but considering his actual desires, he was being Prince fucking Charming.

"Wait. Where?" She tried tugging on him, but he ignored it. He could only imagine what she thought was going to happen, where he was going to make her sleep, but it wasn't as bad as she conjured in her mind.

It wasn't even that late. Hell, the sun had only just slipped away, the sky wasn't even completely dark yet. But he needed her away from him for a few minutes. He needed to sort things out, to get in touch with his guy, to get information and make a plan. Easiest way to do that was to put the girl to bed.

He hurried her up the stairs, through the hallway of the house, and up another flight of stairs to the bedrooms. The contractor had finished his room months ago. When he needed to get away from the city, to hide out, or just cool his heels for a bit, he would come to the farmhouse.

Once in his bedroom he continued to pull her toward his private bath. The finishing touches were still being done, but it worked well enough. "Go to the bathroom." He led her into the room and turned on the lights.

She flipped her hair from her face. "Can you shut the door?"

The corner of his mouth curled up, and he laughed. "No. Go." He leaned against the door jamb, folding his hands over his chest.

"I can't if you're watching me," she huffed, her eyes steady on him now.

"Go." He pulled the door halfway shut, leaving it open enough that he could hear what she was doing. Not that she could really do much. The window was too small to climb through, and they were too high up for her to jump. She peed, flushed, and washed her hands. In that order, and in the right amount of time. Good. She didn't fuck around and make him have to go in there to drag her out.

The door opened, and she looked up at him. She was nearly a whole head shorter, making him tower over her even when he wasn't trying to be persuasive. "It's not late enough to go to bed," she said, jerking her chin toward the bedroom windows. The sun had set, but a dark gray hue still hung in the sky.

"Tell me what's at the post office," he tried once more, hoping the sting in her ass might put some sense in her head.

She sighed and shook her head. "I don't know." But she did, or at least she had an idea. Hell, even he had an idea.

He jerked his thumb toward the king-sized bed. "Get in bed." He walked away from her, keeping an eye on the door, in case she decided running away naked wasn't such a terrible idea.

Some of his things had already been moved from his apartment in Chicago. Grabbing a pair of leather cuffs from his dresser, he met her at the bed. "No, the other side." He pointed to the side furthest from the door.

Throwing him a disgruntled glance, she pushed past him

and walked around the bed. It was his first chance to see her ass. The undersides of her cheeks were still a nice deep red, while a few dark welts crossed her upper thighs and over the lush curves of her ass.

"Hold on, wait." He met up with her just as she pulled the covers back. He gripped her shoulders, feeling the heat of her skin beneath his own. "I want to check your ass."

"Want to admire your handiwork? Asshole." She crossed her arms over her chest, but didn't try to turn around or jump away.

"Peaches, you have no idea what me being an asshole looks like, but if you keep this up, this resistance, this lying, you'll find out. And this little spanking," he patted her ass, feeling the warmth of the spanking, "will seem like child's play."

He let his fingertips roam over the welts. The skin hadn't broken. It would have been pretty hard to do considering she'd been fully clothed at the time, and he'd held back on the strength.

Two hard pats to her ass, and he gave her a little shove. "Go on. Get in and give me your wrists."

She climbed into the bed, quickly pulling the thick quilt up to her chin. A soft blush covered her cheeks—from the spanking, or being nude?

"Hands," he said again, opening one of the wrist cuffs and holding it out for her to put her wrist in.

"You don't have to do that. I'm naked, where the hell am I going to go?" Good point, but it didn't matter. He wanted her in one place and one place only.

He leaned down, his face hovering over hers. Damn, she smelled good; even with the faint scent of motor oil and dirt from the truck bed, he could still smell her sweetness. "You need to learn real quick to do what you're told, the first time. If I have to keep my repeating myself, I'll punish you first. Got it, peaches?"

Her teeth snapped when she shut her mouth, coming to the wise conclusion not to push him. Especially when he was so close to her. She slid her hands up between them and shoved her wrists into his chest. Without looking away from her face, he grasped them and worked the first cuff over her wrist, then the second. Once both were on tightly, he stood back up, dragging her arms over her head and securing her wrists to the low set of D-rings built into the sturdy headboard. He had the playroom built, but that didn't mean he couldn't have just as much fun in his own bedroom.

"What is this place?" she asked when he had her completely secured and checked her wrists to be sure he left enough room for blood flow. He'd check her fingers again when he came to bed. Later. After he figured out what his next step was.

He dragged his gaze down her arms to her dark brown eyes. "My retirement." He leaned toward her. Her lips were wet from her licking them. She was probably thirsty. He should get her something to drink. "It's time for little girls to go to bed."

"I'm not a little girl," she said with narrowed eyes. Such fire from a woman tied up to his bed. He dragged the quilt down, letting her breasts free from the cover.

"No. You're not," he said, cupping one breast. She closed her eyes when he began to roll her nipple between his fingers. "Look at me, peaches. Open your eyes. It's one place that doesn't lie." When she turned her head away from him, he increased the force of his fingers.

When her eyes met his, he nearly lost himself in them. Complete desire and lust swam in her dilated pupils. Lowering himself down, he took the free nipple into his mouth, moaning at the soft salty taste of her skin. Or was that her moan?

Twirling his tongue around the hardened peak, he used his hand to pinch the other nipple, earning a small gasp from his captive. He sucked harder, and harder still until her breasts pulled up away from her body, and she arched her chest trying to lessen the strain.

Her breast fell free of his mouth with a pop, and he

grinned down at her. No trace of the brown irises that were there a moment ago, only dark black pupils signaling how much she enjoyed what he was doing.

He stood up, clearing his throat and tossing the quilt back over her. He had work to do, and ravishing her at that moment wasn't it. No matter how much his cock ached to sink into what had to be her tight, wet pussy. "Get some sleep."

She gave a retort, trying to get back some of her gumption most likely, but he let it go. He had to get his head back on straight and get the job going. He was almost finished, almost done with all the fucking bullshit. He couldn't let her get in his way.

• • • • • • •

What the hell was wrong with her, letting her body react that way to him? He was a kidnapper! Yet there she was swimming in her own fucking juices between her legs because he sucked on her breasts? No, more than that. He took her choice away. He tied her to his bed, and then played with her body as though she were a little toy he found on the floor. And instead of trying to bite him, kick him, or twist away, she had arched upward into his mouth?

After she'd been lying in the bed alone for what felt like forever, Devin had finally come to bed. She didn't open her eyes when the bed sank in beside her. When his bare leg brushed hers under the covers, she yanked her leg away and tried to turn to her side. Her hands were bound low enough on the headboard that she hadn't lost the feeling in them, but they weren't comfortable if she was lying any other way than on her back. He did that on purpose. The bastard.

She listened to him breathing and waited until the heavy, steady breath signaled he'd fallen asleep. Then she began counting the minutes. She couldn't see the clock on the nightstand with him lying next to her, so she made do with what she could, and counted to sixty over and over again.

Losing count several times, she figured enough time had passed. He was deep in sleep.

It was her chance, her only shot at getting it right. He needed to be sleepy, but not too much so that he wouldn't be able to unlock the wrist cuffs.

"Devin," she whispered in his direction. He rolled over, throwing a heavy arm around her stomach. "Devin," she tried again with a louder voice. He pulled her closer to him, snuggling her to his chest. Dammit! "Devin. Wake up." She jammed her foot into his leg. He startled, popped up to his elbows, then set fierce eyes on her. "I have to pee." She tugged on her restraints. "Please. Unlock me. I have to pee bad."

"You went before you got in bed." He laid back down, keeping his arm over her stomach, and resting his face too close to hers. She could smell the mint of the toothpaste he'd used before coming to bed for the night.

"Do you want me to piss the bed?" Crude, yes, but the man didn't seem to understand things any other way.

With a low growl he rolled over and opened a drawer. When he sat over her, he fiddled with the wrist cuffs, unlocking them from the rings, but not taking them off her. Before she could sit up, he brought his nose to touch hers. "Don't do anything stupid." With that, he rolled onto his back.

"I won't. I promise." She scooted off the bed and ran for the bathroom. Thankfully the door had a lock. She flipped it and tested it before going to work. Behind the toilet sat a small toolbox, probably left by the construction workers. She'd noticed it earlier, and prayed there was something in it that would prove helpful.

Carefully, she pulled it out and placed it on the floor; opening the lid, she closed her eyes and said another prayer that there would be help inside. When she opened her eyes she nearly cried out with relief. A knife would have been better, but the shiny flat-head screwdriver would do nicely. From the look of it, it was as close to new as she could hope.

Gripping the handle, she stood up and headed for the door. Taking a deep breath, she stilled herself for what she was going to have to do. There was no mistake it would be hard, but he left her no choice. She couldn't just lie next to him waiting for him to rape her, or kill her. No, she had to get out of there.

A thin layer of sweat covered her palms as she turned the knob, her breath shaky and her mind whirling. She could do this, she could. Tommy told her once, a long time ago, that some situations were kill or be killed, and always in those situations to be killed was not an option.

She opened the door enough to peek out and see him still lying on the bed. The covers were thrown off, giving her a view of his body. He'd stripped out of his shirt and jeans, but left his boxers on. At least he had some modesty.

Taking a tentative step into the room, she waited to see if he moved. Nothing. Still gripping the handle of the screwdriver, harder than before out of fear of dropping it and waking him, she finished walking over to his side of the bed. His eyes were closed—a good sign.

She took in a deep breath and closed both hands over the handle of the screwdriver. His large, muscular chest laid out beneath her gaze. A tattoo played across his chest and over both shoulders, but it was too dark and she was too distracted by the pounding of her own heart to make out the actual design.

Hard thrust. She needed to put all her weight into the thrust or the screwdriver wouldn't be deadly enough. Maybe she could just wound him; surely he wouldn't chase after her with a screwdriver sticking out of his arm or leg. More hard muscles, and another tattoo wound around his left thigh. Fuck. She needed to stop looking at him and just do it.

Raising up the screwdriver over her head, she closed her eyes, ready to bring it down right into his chest. "I wouldn't do it." His almost whispered sentence startled her. Panic rose in her throat as well as bile. She brought her hands down hard, slashing at him.

The screwdriver bit into flesh; he yelled then shoved at her. She dropped her hands and stumbled backwards, trying to see where she snagged him. Deciding better to run than check it out, she turned and took off for the door.

She twisted the doorknob. It turned easily but the door wouldn't open. She cried out in frustration and continued to tug on the unlocked door. "Come on!" she screamed, pounding her fist into the door "Fucking open!" She tugged harder, looking over her shoulder and hoping to see him still on the bed.

Stone cold eyes met hers. Only a breath away. His hand jutted out and grabbed her hair. Too easily, he pulled her back and she fell to the floor. She crab-crawled backwards, as though a few feet of distance would protect her from his fury.

Moonlight poured in through the window, bathing his body in the white glow. A gash on his left bicep caught her eye. Not large, and not as much blood as she would have thought, but it was something. Unfortunately, he was right-handed.

She watched with a panicked breath as he reached up and slid the security bolt open at the top of the door. Noticing that one, she also noticed two others that had been unlocked. Why hadn't she taken more time to look around the room before attempting to run from it?

Still in retreat mode, she scrambled further until her back hit the bed. It was with little effort that he reached her and hauled her up to her feet. Expecting his hand to take a vise grip on her arm again, she was surprised when his shoulder dug into her stomach, and she was tossed over his shoulder like a sack of flour.

The door flew open, and she saw stairs bouncing beneath her vision. "No! No!" She began to kick, squirm, pound her fists into his broad back, but none of it deterred him. The stairs disappeared, replaced with floor boards. She tried to reach out to the wall, to grab a door jamb, something to make him stop. He wasn't saying anything; he didn't even slap her when she punched his back. Where the hell was he taking her?

Kitchen tile came into view, and she increased her attempt to escape his hold. He was taking her downstairs. To the discipline room. Where the walls were covered in implements, and there were so many ways for him to tie her down for a beating. He warned her, and she'd gambled with the damn screwdriver.

She should have been stronger. Not thought so much and had just done it. Maybe he wouldn't have realized her intent, maybe she could have gotten away.

"Stop!" she cried when another door creaked open and his feet padded down the wooden steps. "No!" She drew out her nails, dragging them up his bare back, digging into him as hard as she could. It was too late.

They were downstairs, and even though he growled at her assault it hadn't stopped him, hadn't even paused his step.

She heard metal grating against metal, and before she realized where he'd taken her, he'd flung her off his shoulder and dumped her on the floor. Looking up, she saw the black barred door shut, heard the bang of the lock taking hold and she bolted for the door, yanking on it. "No!" She pulled harder, unable to allow herself to believe she was truly locked in a cage.

He took a step back from the cage, his chest heaving from his heavy breath. A light had been flicked on somewhere along the way, giving enough light for her to make out his face. She wished it hadn't.

"Let me out!"

He didn't say anything. He still wasn't speaking, just catching his breath with his hands balled into fists at his sides. Every muscle in his body clenched with his anger. The wound she inflicted had already stopped bleeding, and in the light it looked like she'd only scratched him. He turned away from her, giving her a chance to see the work of her nails on his flesh, and headed up the stairs. Still saying nothing.

"Devin! No! No!" She rattled the cage more, slapping her hands at the bars. "Don't leave me down here! Please! I'm sorry!" What did he expect? That she'd remain a docile little captive? "Please!"

Her answer came a moment later. The lights went out, and the door shut upstairs. "No," she whispered, resting her forehead against the cool metal of the cage. "Please."

Tears welled in her eyes. Not having the energy to wipe them away, or to hold them back, she let them fall. For the first time since she'd opened her eyes to find Devin in her apartment, she let the horror and fear of the day seep into her bones.

In the corner of the cell was a folded blanket and a pillow. Had he been planning on putting her in the damn thing from the beginning? She grabbed the blanket and wrapped it around her naked body before sinking to the floor and leaning against the bars.

She had been kidnapped, spanked twice, tied up and thrown in a trunk, dragged to some unknown farmhouse. No one knew where she was, or even why she'd gone missing. Dr. Conrad might worry; she'd never been late to work, much less miss an entire day without calling. But would he really do anything to check on her? Julie might stop at her apartment, but when there wasn't an answer, would she keep trying?

For years she'd kept people at bay, not making friends, not making relationships work. All because she didn't want the complications that came with them. Trying to get her own big brother to fly straight took up almost all of her energy, and showed her how devastatingly disappointing people could be. And what did all that protection she gave herself get her? Locked in a cell in some crazy man's basement without anyone who would even notice she disappeared.

And the worst part of it, at that very moment, the

moment she let herself feel sorry for her situation, her bladder poked her.

She needed to pee.

CHAPTER SIX

Sunlight filtered through the bathroom window, nearly blinding Devin as he stepped out of the shower. He needed to get some drapes in there, something to block out that damn sun. Grabbing a towel from the rack, he went about drying off. Raking the towel through his short tresses, he caught a glimpse of his arm in the mirror.

Kara didn't get a good chunk out of his arm, but enough for it be stiff and annoying in the morning. The fucking toolbox. He hadn't seen it tucked behind the toilet. When he heard the bathroom door open and didn't hear her move toward the bed, he knew something was wrong. He'd kept still, watched her through narrowly opened eyes. He'd seen the screwdriver in her hands, but didn't move. Maybe he wanted to see if she had it in her, or maybe he doubted her intentions. Either way, she damn near got a good stab into him.

He'd have to deal with her now. Her claws were fully exposed, and he was running out of time. He'd dragged himself to bed the night before after too many calls, too many questions, and not enough answers to appease anyone who mattered. If he didn't get to the bottom of what damage that woman could do, she'd have more to worry about than just him. Tommy had made a big fucking mess and if Devin didn't play this right, Kara would be the one mopping it all up.

He shouldn't care about that. Get the information, take care of the loose ends, and end the fucking job. Move on into retirement and start his new life.

But those eyes of hers. His mother had the same eyes. Hard and fearless when protecting her kids, and had the ability to melt like butter to soften up everyone around her. He hadn't been able to protect her though, not from his drunken father, or from the harshness of working double shifts too many days a week, and not from that asshole who saw her as another set of eyes that didn't need to be seeing.

Tossing the towel back on the rack, he walked through the bedroom naked, stretching his muscles as he went to his dresser. Who knew manhandling such a small woman could use so much energy. It had been on pure adrenaline that he carried her down to that cage. Even her nails digging into his back hadn't waylaid him, though he felt the burn of those scratches well enough in the shower. He'd have to cut those damn nails off, first thing.

Yes, a shower and grooming. That might help get her to cooperate, or at least start to understand her position.

After getting dressed in a clean pair of jeans and a t-shirt, he laced up his boots and headed down to the kitchen. No point on working with her on an empty stomach; he just hoped that the groceries he'd had delivered to the house the week before were still edible. The crew wrapped up a week before, and Devin had made sure there was always food in the kitchen for the men. And for himself when he popped up there from time to time.

While he cooked up some eggs for himself, he opened the door to the basement. Listening for sounds of her movement, he finished plating up the scrambled eggs. Eating them while standing in the doorway, he wondered if she could smell the aroma of his breakfast. He had thought about coffee, but he had a schedule to keep and didn't have time for the luxury.

"Devin?" A soft plea sailed up the stairs. "Devin, I need to use the washroom."

He shook his head. Did she think he'd fall for that lie twice? She needed to work on her creativity.

"I mean it. Really."

He put his plate down on the counter nearest him and shut the door. The frustrated groan he heard made his smile widen. He went to the kitchen pantry and dug out what he wanted, then headed down to the basement.

Kara stood at the door of the cage, blanket wrapped around her in toga fashion, gripping the bars. She looked from him to the bucket he held in his hand and her hopeful eyes drooped. "What's that for?" she asked.

"Go stand at the back of your cage." He pointed to the far corner, where the pillow still lay on the floor, exactly where he'd left it and looked unused. Had she slept at all?

Once she shuffled to the correct spot, he unlocked the door and opened it, dropping the metal bucket onto the floor. "Your bathroom." He pointed to it, and shut the door again, locking it securely.

She looked at the rusted metal then back to him. "Devin. Please. I'm sorry."

"Not yet, but you will be. You see, your little stunt last night took away all privileges. Forget your clothes, forget the comfort of a bed, forget using a fucking toilet. Now take your piss; we have things to do."

"Devin." The whispered plea didn't work on him, not when his arm throbbed and his back burned. Hell, no. She'd piss in that bucket and that was the end of it.

He looked at his watch and tsked his tongue. "I have about one hour before I have to get my shit going, so if I were you, I'd hurry the fuck up if you want to wash off the grime of the truck and sweat from all that running around you did."

At the prospect of a shower, she eyed the bucket with a bit more appreciation. She shot him another pleading look as she stepped toward the bucket, but he wasn't going to let those big doe eyes and pouting lips sway him. Even the streaks of dried tears down her cheeks did nothing but make his dick hard again. Fuck. This girl didn't know how much she got to him, how under his skin she was getting. When he'd first seen her with Tommy he pegged her for the girl next door, sweet innocent type. But no. The girl had fire and ice running through her insides. Just thinking about it made his cock push the limit of his zipper.

He kept silent while she picked up the bucket and took it to the back corner. She kept the blanket wrapped around her as best she could while squatting over her chamber pot. He never let his eyes wander away while the slow trickle began and her bladder emptied. She needed to feel his gaze hot on her back, burning her flesh with his stare. There would be no privacy, no moments to collect herself; when he wanted something from her, she was damn well going to give it to him right away.

When she was finished, she looked around, trying to find something to wipe herself with, no doubt. "Finish up, and grab the bucket." He swung the door to the cage open again. "Time to get cleaned up." He stopped her when she tried to straighten out the blanket. "Take that off, and leave it here. It's to cover you when you sleep, not cover you from my eyes. You use it as a dress again, and I'll take it away."

Hot eyes shot at him, but she didn't argue. She peeled away the fleece blanket and dropped it on top of the pillow. When she started to walk toward him empty-handed, he stopped her again and pointed to the bucket. "I'm not your chambermaid."

She picked up the bucket and walked toward him, a glint in her eye that suggested what she was thinking. Lucky for her she thought better once her eyes lifted to his face. That would be the worst thing she could do at that moment. If so much of a drop hit him, he'd take her over to the bench and strap her down, not letting her up until she'd tasted every last implement he had in the place. She must have seen the warning in his expression, because she carefully carried the bucket past him and headed toward the stairs.

"Wait." She paused with one foot on the first step and looked back at him. He went to the set of drawers built into the wall and opened the top one. Pulling out a thin leather collar and the matching lead, he shut the drawer and headed back to her.

"Devin. No." She tried to step away but there wasn't anywhere for her to go. He slipped the adjustable collar around her neck and tightened it. Running a quick finger along the inside of the leather piece, grazing her neck to be sure there was enough room, he gave her a nod.

"Can't really trust you, now can I?" He stepped around her and gave the strip of leather a little tug to get her moving.

He pulled her along through the kitchen and out the back door. Five steps down from the porch and they were standing in the wooded back yard. He planned to clear some of the area away to make for a BBQ pit area, but the remodel hadn't begun back there yet.

Tugging on the leash, he brought her to a tree a few hundred yards from the house. "Dump it here." He pointed to the ground.

Her cheeks reddened and her hands shook a bit, but she managed to tip the bucket over and empty the contents into the grass, stepping back to avoid any splatter onto her bare feet.

"I'd be good if I were you or lose the privilege of having the bucket. Be a shame if you had to be walked out here to take a leak every time, right?" He didn't see her reaction to that threat, because he'd gotten busy tying the end of the leash to a thick limb overhead.

Satisfied the knot would hold against any resistance she might give, he turned back to her, wiping his hands on his jeans. He grabbed her wrists before she could think to pull away and used the clasps on the leather rings to hook them onto the leash. She looked miserable. Her hair was tangled a bit in the back; maybe she had slept. And fitfully so.

He checked the tensions again, making sure she wouldn't get herself hung when she struggled to stay still, then clapped his hands together.

"Time for your shower." He grinned and started to head back toward the house.

"Here?" she called to him, and he didn't bother responding. He'd just tied her to a fucking tree, where did she think she was having it?

It was pretty warm for a fall day, which was good—for her.

Her eyes widened and her mouth dropped open when he headed back toward her carrying the hose in one hand and a bucket in the other.

"No. No. Not a hose."

Funny how she thought she had the right to demand anything from him at that moment. After she'd sliced him. After she'd spit at him. After she'd fought and clawed at him. Between the two of them, she had been the most violent.

"Oh, yes, the hose. That's how I clean my pets, peaches." Her intake of breath at how he referred to her wasn't lost on him. Such a little sound really. Most men wouldn't even notice it, but not Devin. No, he not only noticed it, he basked in those little sounds. The hums, the shocked gasps, the painful cries, the soft murmurs of pleasure, all if it stroked his arousal to an almost painful point.

"I-I'm sorry if I hurt you." Her apology came fast, her eyes never leaving the bucket as he began to fill it with water. A bar of soap floated in the chilly water along with a rag he'd tossed in there. He was going to enjoy cleaning her.

"I'm sure you are," he agreed, tilting his head to look up at her. "That doesn't change much, though, I'm afraid. You see, actions have consequences." He lifted up his left arm, where the injury was hidden beneath the sleeve of his t-shirt. "Even when you're sorry. I'll give you a word of advice.

Take your punishment like a good girl, and you'll start earning your privileges back." Bubbles formed in the water, and he turned off the spray from the hose, closing the gap between them.

"Just let me go. I just want to go home." She stomped her foot in the dirt. Her bare foot made no sound against the earth beneath it, but the dirt kicked up a bit. He looked down at the few particles that landed on his boot.

"Now you're kicking dirt at me?" It was cruel to add that to her list of transgressions, but the beast within him was slowly making its way off its leash.

"No." Her curls flew from side to side as she shook her head. "No, Please. I—" She screamed when the cold water from the hose hit her naked body. She jumped back, but the leash didn't give her much room to move away.

"What was that?"

She twisted away, but the water caught her. "C-cold! Too cold!" she screamed.

"I bet it is," he nodded in agreement, aiming the hose for her chest. Her nipples tightened into stiff peaks with the chilled water hitting her. He couldn't have planned for a sexier sight. She tried to close her arms, to protect her breasts, but they were tied overhead. He softened the stream and stepped closer, watching the water fall over her heavy breasts and roll down her flat stomach toward that little patch of hair he had admired earlier. He let go of the handle, stopping the water for a moment. "Turn around. I want to get your back."

"No!" she refused.

He turned the water back on and aimed the stream at her hardened nipples. She squealed, twisted, and turned, but couldn't get away from him. Damn, his dick was hard.

"Turn around." He gave her another chance, aiming the stream to the side.

"I hate you," she affirmed once more, then slowly turned so her ass faced him.

He nearly groaned at the sight of her round ass. Only a

few welts were still showing from the belting he'd given her the night before, but other than that her creamy skin was completely unflawed. Of course he'd remedy that after her shower. The girl still had a punishment coming. A hard punishment.

"You can hate me all you want. Won't change what's coming." He rinsed off her back then stepped closer, wrapping his hand to her front and cupping her chin. Pulling it back, he began to gently spray her hair. Her breath hitched, but soon adjusted to the new chill. "Now you need soap," he whispered in her ear.

Gathering the soap and washcloth, he went back over to her. Her body shivered a bit, and she rested her head against her arm, steeling herself for what was coming.

Deciding against the washcloth, he tossed it back in the bucket and lathered up his hands. She tried to cow away as he reached for her, but the leather pulled on her, and she had to step forward again. He washed her thoroughly, not missing a spot on her body. He paid special attention to her breasts, holding them and caressing the heavy globes. She tried to hide her face, but he saw her eyes when he ran his thumbs over her nipples. He heard that little gasp when his fingers slid between her pussy lips. Her legs parted all on their own when he started to reach her pussy.

"Ah, there you go." His fingers found her clit, already swollen and probably wet from more than just the hosing he gave her.

She clenched her eyes shut. As though that would keep her from feeling what he was giving her. If her eyes hadn't been so dilated, if her breath hadn't given her away, he would have thought maybe it was just a natural bodily effect. Stroking her clit would arouse her simply because it was the job of her clit to act in that way. But the other tells were there, and before he even reached her little nub.

She liked what he was doing; she liked the objectification, the loss of control.

Well, fuck. He'd already suspected, but to see it

firsthand—his cock couldn't get any harder without injury.

"All lathered up." He gave her hip a light slap and walked around her, reaching for her hair. "I don't have any fancy soaps for you to use, at least not until you've earned it." He lathered his hands back up and dove into her hair, running his fingers through the wet tangles. "Don't have a brush either; well, I do, but it's not meant for brushing hair."

"It's used for more beatings?" she shot at him over her shoulder. A momentary defiance. Easily squashed.

He spun her around to face him and cupped her face in his hands, forcing her to keep looking at him. "I have never, nor will I ever, beat a woman." A truth so loud, so real, his chest hurt speaking it. Beating was what his old man did. And he was nothing like his old man.

Devin ran his thumb over her bottom lip, looking deep into her dark eyes. "Now, your brother's friends. I don't think I can say the same about them." It had taken everything in Devin not to shoot the bastards when he'd witnessed how they handled their girls.

"Tommy wouldn't have allowed that." The statement given with a hard edge, but beneath it, in her eyes, he could see she wasn't entirely sure. Although her skepticism was correct, he felt a twinge of regret at having placed it there. Tommy had been all she had; some things didn't need to be dragged into the light.

His thumb traced her upper lip. "There are things you don't need to know. But it's what you do know that I'm interested in, peaches. You wanna tell me now? Save yourself some trouble?"

Before she could answer, he brought his mouth down on hers. Covering hers completely. He expected resistance, possibly even for her to try biting him. What he didn't expect was for her lean into him, to part her lips so easily when his tongue lashed against them. His hands moved from her face to her breasts, fondling them as he deepened the kiss. Capturing her as much in that moment as he had when he took her from her apartment.

When he pulled back, looking down at her, he smiled. A soft blush had taken over her cheeks, her eyes were searching his face, but her mouth clamped shut. She was ashamed. She hadn't meant to enjoy that.

"Time to rinse off." He released her and grabbed the bucket, tipping it over her head. She danced and screamed as the water poured over her body. There had been some suds in the bucket, but she was mostly rinsed off. Good enough for the next portion of the morning events. "Be right back. Stay here." He winked and headed to the small shed a few yards away from the house.

•••••••

Kara leaned her head against her arm, gulping in air. Shivers ran through her body as the light breeze chilled her even more than the water had. Her hair clung to her face, and her nipples hardened to the point of pain.

He'd kissed her. His tongue had been in her mouth, dancing with hers; worse yet, she'd liked it. A simple body response, she told herself. He'd been fondling her just moments before, whispering into her ear. It was natural for her body to react to him.

It was obvious the man had experience. His fingers played her clit too easily, his kiss stole her breath too quickly. She needed to get a grip and fast. Just because someone played with her breasts, stroked her clit, and kissed her with pure possession, didn't give her a reason to start acting like some whore.

He was her kidnapper. He'd stolen her from her apartment, her life. He'd forced her to pee in a bucket, for crying out loud. No. She would not react to anything else he did. She would remain stoic. Completely unattached to whatever he threw her way.

Confidence is a finicky thing. Easily pushed away when one sees a man stalking toward you with what looked like a razor strap. She'd seen a few of those in her internet travels, and never did she see anyone say how pleasant they were. No. It was a punishment implement. Not used for play, at least not light play.

The cold was no longer the only reason her flesh trembled.

"Devin." She twisted to look at him, aiming her ass away. "Please. I'm sorry. I said I was sorry."

"We already had that conversation," he sighed, tapping the strap against his thigh. Little water marks were splattered across the light denim from the shower he'd given her. "What did I say?"

She yanked at her bonds over her head; they wouldn't give. He'd been too masterful in his knot tying, the leather too strong; running from him wasn't really an option.

"You said actions have consequences." Even to her own ears she sounded pitiful. He was going use that damn thing on her; she deserved to sound pitiful.

"Good girl. You were listening." He smiled, a genuine smile and stood right in front of her. "Keep being a good girl, and maybe you'll get to pee in the bathroom today." The reminder of having to piss in that damn bucket brought back the heated blush across her face. Damn him. Damn him to hell. Humiliation wasn't enough; he needed to inflict physical pain.

He stepped out of her eyesight, but she could hear him behind her. Fingers lightly traced across her ass, eliciting a soft burn from where his belt had struck her the day before.

"I trusted you to use the bathroom and come back to bed. You betrayed that trust," he stated flatly, dropping his fingers from her flesh. Her ass twitched at his abandonment.

"You kidnapped me!" she yelled out into the air. Did anyone live close enough to hear her? He hadn't seemed concerned when she'd screamed during the shower. "Why the fuck would I not try to get away?"

A sharp slap crossed her right cheek. Not the strap, his hand. She jumped from the surprise. "Your mouth is filthy, maybe I need to clean that, too?" He pointed to the bar of soap nestled in the grass near the bucket.

"You curse all the time!" She eyed the soap while arguing with him.

"There's a big difference, pet. I will say when you get to have a filthy mouth and when you don't. And while you're being punished, you don't. Now, should I help you clean up your language?"

She clamped her mouth shut and shook her head.

"I'm trying to help you, peaches. If you are going to get out of this mess, you'll have to start helping me do that. You need to start being good, and being honest."

She felt him moving behind her, but she couldn't see him, nor did she strain herself to try. That strap in his hand gave off wicked vibes, and nothing in her past fantasies was going to prepare her for what was coming. She clenched her buttocks, squeezed her eyes shut, and held her breath, waiting for the first blow.

When it didn't come, she eased her eyes open and softened her muscles. Had he changed his mind?

A throat-burning scream unleashed from her body the moment the thick leather brought down a fiery stripe across her ass. Never had she experienced such intense pain in such a short time. Acute burning. Before she could regain her composure, he brought it down again, a little lower but still on her ass, still overlapping the flaming strike before it.

"I did tell you that you'd regret it if you were a bad girl, didn't I, peaches?" He didn't wait for her to answer; he brought the strap down again. Her eyes clenched tight, squeezing the tears out, letting them fall down her cheeks.

Another scorching blow, and she jumped forward, feeling the collar around her neck chafe, but preferring that to the unreal pain in her ass.

He wrapped an arm around her waist and picked her up off the ground. "That won't do, Kara. No hurting yourself, or I'll have to add more to your punishment." He walked back a few paces and put her back on the ground, keeping his arm wrapped around her waist. His breath washed against her cheek as he rested his chin on her shoulder. "I knew I would like the sound of your screams, but I really didn't think I'd love it so much. You make such pretty sounds, and I'm sure your body is loving it, too."

"No." She shook her head gently, careful not to bump into him. "Please, Devin. Please, no more. I don't like it, I really don't." Tears ran down her cheeks, her eyes burned from them.

"Hmm..." His hand unraveled from around her torso and slid down her still damp body to her pussy, where her own body betrayed her. His fingers slid through her folds with no trouble, and her clit shot a bolt of electric heat through her core when he circled it with his middle finger. "Lying is an entirely new offense, peaches, but I'll let it go this time. You don't want to like this, but you do." He released her clit. "And so do I."

With his hand gone, his arm gone, an emptiness replaced them. She rolled her head to the side, resting it on her arm, taking the reprieve to catch her breath. He wouldn't have it. Another strike, and another. The sound of the leather slapping against her cheeks echoed in her mind. Trying to time his strokes, she clenched her body. It did nothing. Every fiber in her soul could feel the burn of that strap. He wasn't talking anymore, wasn't touching her, only whipping her with the instrument of the devil.

"Stop! Please!" Her throat was raw, her mouth completely dry, but he ignored her plea.

"You need to learn, Kara. I won't tolerate disobedience." Another hard hit and her knees buckled beneath her. He caught her, pulling her up to her feet, and she leaned back against him.

His chest pressed against her back, the strength of his muscles giving her back what he'd taken from her. Her tears flowed freely, her shoulders shook, but she didn't care. The ache in her arms, the fire in her ass, everything hurt beyond what she thought she could bear.

"Shhh..." He wrapped another arm around her, hugging

her to him. His lips nuzzled into her neck, kissing her. "You did so good, pet. So good." He kissed her earlobe, then her cheek.

"Please," she whispered, still not looking at him.

"Please what, pet?" One hand splayed out across her belly, slowly sinking back to where her heat displayed her body's treachery. "You'll have to ask for what you want, and ask nicely or you won't get it." His words sank into her body. What she wanted, what did she want? No, she wouldn't ask him for that. Never would she ask him to put out the fire he'd stirred up inside her.

"I hurt." Simple, and not a lie. She did hurt, everywhere. Some places from the strapping, others from neglect.

His hand inched lower, the tip of his finger brushing through the bit of hair she kept when she last trimmed. "I like this little patch here." He patted the soft curls, now wet with her own arousal as much as the shower. "What do you want, pet?"

"Make it stop." She leaned her head back against his body when one finger pressed down on her clit. Fuck, that's exactly what she needed. But from him? Not from him, this wasn't supposed to be happening with him.

"How do you ask nicely, pet?"

"Please. Please make it stop." If she hadn't heard her own words she wouldn't have believed she'd said it. Begging him to touch her hadn't even been that difficult.

He slid his hand even lower, between her legs. Two fingers toyed with her entrance and like the whore he was turning her into, she parted her legs for him. The heel of his hand rubbed against her clit as the fingers thrust into her, filling her. Too many sensations, but not enough at the same time.

"There's the sound," he whispered into her ear after she moaned.

Behind her, his cock pressed through his jeans onto her ass. Denim rubbing her raw ass burned, almost as much as the strike itself and he knew it. He pushed his cock harder against her and she wiggled. "Do you feel that, pet?"

She wouldn't answer him, couldn't answer him while he pumped his fingers into her harder and with more speed, driving her head first toward her orgasm. But actions have consequences, natural or otherwise.

His hand pulled free, and slapped her pussy hard. She cried out and tried to close her legs, but he slapped her again twice. "Open your legs," he ordered with a smack to her thighs. She walked her feet apart. "Answer me. Do you feel my cock pressing against your ass?"

"Y-yes." She nodded. His hand covered her pussy, pushing her backward onto his cock, making her opening clench. She wanted his fingers back, wanted her clit touched, and the fire in her ass to subside long enough for her brain to start working again.

"Tell me what you feel, what you want." His breath was so hot against her ear, making her hungrier for what he was offering. The muscles of his chest moved as his hand began to stroke her pussy, pet it as he would a…well, a pet. And isn't that what he called her now? His pet?

She wanted his lips back on her, the warmth and power of his kiss, but she wouldn't give him that. No, a kiss was too intimate, gave him too much power.

"Your cock." She gave him a side glance and saw the smile creep over his lips. When he smiled, genuinely smiled, he could be devastating, and in that moment, he looked pleased as hell.

"Good girl." He tossed the leather strap onto the ground, and used his hand to maneuver behind her. The zipper came down, the button undone, fabric bustled. He pushed her chest forward, just enough to put a bend in her body, but not enough to tighten the collar around her neck.

The rounded, smooth tip of his dick slid between her raw cheeks, pressing to the entrance of her core. Gripping the leash with her hands, she leveraged herself to arch her back more, to make it easier, to take his cock as he would give it. She held no misgivings that she would in any way be given control in this undertaking. He would give, and she would take. It would be that simple. That's what Devin was. That's how he did things.

He'd wanted to teach her something, and he had. He wouldn't be moved. He would do as he saw fit, when he wanted to, and how he deemed it would be done. And in that moment, at that very precise second that his cock pushed into her warm, wet sheath, she wouldn't have it any other way. Knowing it was wrong, knowing it was only a momentary thing, she leaned back into him, taking the harshness of what he gave.

"That's it, pet." A hand clasped the collar at her nape. "Fuck, you're tight. So tight and hot. Your pussy is drenched for me." He pulled back, inch by incredible inch he pulled away until he was almost all the way out. The fear of being abandoned clenched her pussy. "Ah, there it is, your cunt wants my cock. That's a good pet." The leather pulled back on her throat, tightening around her neck. Breathing became harder, more labored, the pressure against her trachea built along with the pressure in her pussy.

His hand left her clit and grabbed at her thigh, lifting her leg and hooking it over his arm. Now standing on one leg, the collar tight around her throat, with his cock pummeling her hard, her entire insides bloated with pleasure. The intensity rose everywhere. Her fingers holding the leather above her burned as she was jostled from the fucking he gave her, her tits swayed hard with each of his thrusts. Each groan that escaped him as he plowed into her stroked her clit as easily as his fingers had.

"Good pet," he crooned, kissing her shoulder just before biting it. "Now. Tell your owner what you were looking for at the post office. What's there?"

Her mind didn't register; his words came from a foreign tongue. What post office? His cock began to slow, giving her long steady strokes. It wasn't enough, not nearly enough. The collar bit at her neck, cutting off enough air to make her insides melt to his desires, to his will. Breathe or not breathe, it was for him to decide.

Again her clit was petted, being manipulated and pinched, her leg dropped lower on his arm with his new position. The collar tightened against her neck, giving her a new heat, and again his cock thrust upward into her. She held onto the leather leash, hoping not to topple over from standing on one leg.

She couldn't stand the pleasure, it hurt almost as much as the strap. To be dangled so close to the edge, but not being let over the rail. His jeans still rubbed against her sore ass. He hadn't pulled them down. "Please. Oh, please," she begged. For what? To come? At his hand? She'd lost her mind.

"Tell me, pet, and you can come. If you don't, if you defy me, that strap right over there. Look at it."

She opened her eyes and her ass clenched just from the sight of the thick leather staring back up at her, mocking her. Another round of the strap wasn't happening; she couldn't take it. She couldn't stand being on the edge of heaven either.

"Tommy said to go there, left me a box or something." She gasped when his fingers began working her clit harder, driving her forward, his cock pumped harder. "Said if something happened to go get it." She cried out as he held her pelvis back toward him; the denim ripped across her swollen ass, but the new angle sent his cock in a new direction, sucking the breath out of her. So full, so fucking wonderfully full, she couldn't stand it much longer. "Please, Devin. Please," she begged; she'd promise anything at that moment. He worked her body as though it were an extension of his own.

"That's a good pet." He kissed her neck, sucking lightly as he pulled back on the strap of leather around her neck. "Come for me, peaches, come now." Another flick of his finger, a strong thrust of his cock, and she screamed into the sky as the most intense orgasm she'd ever encountered ripped through her body. Muscles tensed, shook, and released with each wave. He continued pumping, harder and harder, the strip around her neck got a little tighter. She struggled for breath as her orgasm began to subside. "Again. Come again," he ordered and stroked her clit harder, in faster circles.

"I-I can't," she groaned out, taking air when she could.

"You will."

Just by his sheer words and the glory of his fingers, her body shook a second time. It had never been possible before, two orgasms in a row, and so intense her vision clouded over. Sparkles were floating in front of her as she yelled out the second orgasm. The leather slackened, he dropped her leg and gripped her hips hard.

The digging of his fingers into her flesh kept her afloat as he fucked her even harder, given the better positioning. He rocked into her. "Good pet. Good girl." He slapped her hip, sending another wave of heat through her already flaming ass. Another strike to her ass, another thrust and he stilled behind her, resting his head on her back, letting loose a low muttering of curses as come burst from his cock into her pussy.

She'd never felt a man come inside of her before. Every little pulse of his orgasm bumped against the walls of her vagina. He hadn't used a condom. Thank god for her birth control shot.

He pulled out of her, making sure she was steady on her feet before he walked away. Grabbing the rag he'd left by the bucket earlier, he cleaned himself off, then saw to her. The cool rag on her pussy soothed some of the heat away, but didn't cure the ache she felt deep inside.

Without a word, he unhooked her cuffs from the rope and worked the knot loose on the tree limb. "C'mon." He gave the rope a little yank to get her moving, snatching her bucket on the way. On unsteady legs she followed him toward the house, her mind reeling with what they had just done.

By the time they reached the porch, he looked over his

shoulder and paused. She wasn't sure what she'd done wrong, but his eyebrows were furrowed, and his eyes were dark again. Hadn't she given him what he wanted? Told him the truth? She tried to step back when he reached for her, but he was faster, and she found herself hauled up in his arms, being carried toward the house cradled in his arms.

He walked through the kitchen and down the steps back to the basement. She whimpered softly into his neck, trying to find comfort in his arms, in his now familiar scent of soap and musk, but she caught a glimpse of the cage and felt the tears begging to burn her eyes again.

Devin carefully put her down on the floor in the cage. "Lie down," he ordered with a pointed finger at the pillow. He unclipped the leash from the collar, but left the leather strap around her neck. "Get some sleep." He covered her with the blanket and walked out of the cell. She closed her eyes at the sound of the metal clanking closed and the lock sliding into place.

Only when she heard the door upstairs close did she open them again and let the tears fall freely again. She'd given in. She'd lost the battle and for what? An orgasm? She kicked her leg out in frustration and grimaced at the sound of the metal bucket being knocked over. He'd brought her pee bucket back in the cell with her. She'd given him what he wanted, and he had locked her back up.

She really was his pet.

CHAPTER SEVEN

Self-discipline and restraint. The military had pressed those traits into Devin during his trainings. None of them had prepared him for Kara's reaction to her punishment, though.

Kara deserved the tanning he gave her; he held no guilt about that. She'd tried to kill him after all; that warranted worse than the few strokes he gave her. He would have finished the strapping if she hadn't stumbled. When he caught her, their bodies mingled together for a moment, and it was just enough for his resolve to crack. Though she probably didn't see it that way. She probably thought she'd received the full dose of her punishment.

Her cries, her tears, the sight of the beautiful ass bucking beneath the strap was too much for one man to take. And when he smelled her arousal, it was finished. He hadn't planned to fuck her. It was a bastard thing to do. It went against the plan, against him, but he had. He'd seen that line coming and jumped right the fuck over it and didn't even look back at it.

Kara didn't know half of what she thought she knew, even when it came to her own brother. Tommy tried to protect her, to keep her from falling into the hands of the evil bastards he surrounded himself with. She thought he killed her brother. Not completely true, but not exactly a lie either. He played his own part in the way things went down.

Tommy had given her something, put something away for her in case of the exact situation she found herself in. He doubted she had any clue as to what was in that post office box, probably hoped it was money. He knew her financial struggle, knew the private funeral she gave her brother had wiped her out. A private funeral that only a few of Cardone's low-level men had attended. That's how Tommy ran things, kept his head ducked and stayed under the radar. Earned his share, remaining under the protection of the Cardone family while being low enough on the totem pole not to attract any unwanted attention to his full dealings.

After taking a quick shower and changing clothes, he ran out to his truck. He grabbed the bag he'd packed for her and brought it into the house. She'd been at Tommy's not long before he popped up for his surprise visit. If she knew about the post office box, she was probably looking for more. Tossing the bag onto the kitchen table, he began digging around through the clothes until he found the purse he'd snatched on the way out.

Sure enough, tucked in her wallet was a small golden key with a four-digit number etched on it. She'd found the key, or maybe she had it all along and was searching his place for something else. He'd find out later. If he was going to get her through this unscathed, he needed to get to that box.

It couldn't be a coincidence that the post office Tommy chose was only two towns over from the farmhouse. He never told Tommy about the farmhouse, he never told anyone, but if Tommy had found out somehow, that meant Michael could know, and if that bastard knew, they were both in danger. Better to get to the box and figure out what the next step was right away.

He quietly opened the basement door to listen. No crying. That was a good sign. Her ass probably still hurt, but it sounded like she was sleeping. Good. Taking her out would be too dangerous. She couldn't be trusted not to try to run or talk to someone. No, she would stay where it was safe for her.

Locked in her cage.

The drive to Eagle didn't take long. Barely used country roads were a pleasant change from all the traffic in Chicago. The day he said goodbye to the city for good would be the best day of his life.

As he pulled into the post office his phone started ringing. Knowing putting off the inevitable any longer would only make things harder, he answered.

"Where's the fucking girl?" Michael Cardone was never much for pleasantries. Right to the point with him.

"I have her. Relax." Devin leaned back against the headrest. The ache behind his eyes was starting to spread up into his head.

"She have the stuff?" Michael inhaled off a cigarette. The man was a chimney when not stressed; having this all hanging over his head made it even worse.

"I'm looking for it. I don't think she knows about it." Innocence meant nothing to men like Michael Cardone.

"Well, get the shit and take care of her. Same way her brother went out."

"Kinda hard stuff for an innocent, dontcha think?" Devin pinched the bridge of his nose, forcing himself to sound aloof. No way Kara was seeing the end of her life the way her brother had.

"You questioning me? She's a fucking rat, and all rats go down the same way."

She was a rat. An unwilling, unknowing rat, but Michael wouldn't stop to take stock of all the facts. Kill now, question later, if at all. "Nah, no questions. You want it that way, you got it. You're the boss." Just saying the words turned his stomach, but no sense in giving everything away too quickly. This was his last dealing with Michael Cardone, even if he didn't know it yet.

"Make sure you remember that." The disgust in his tone didn't go unnoticed. The last year spent working with the Cardone family hadn't been easy to stomach. The whole bunch were a few cards short of a full deck, but he'd made it work. He stayed under the big radars, did what he was told, and got the job done. Now that it was at the end, he just wanted the whole thing over with. Too much time and energy being poured into people he wouldn't take the time to spit on if they were sitting in a drought. "Is she as cute as I remember?" The lewd sneer seeped through the phone waves. "Tommy hid the bitch well enough, but I remember once when I went to his place to pick him up for a job, she was there. Giving him a hard time about leaving, too. Kept trying to shove want ads at him. Fucking bitch, like he'd make money doing anything else. A real control freak, that little sister of his." He had her pegged, partially right. Controlling, probably. The woman saw the world as her responsibility, at least when it had come to Tommy. Whoever heard of the little sister, nearly a decade younger, trying over and over again to take care of her big brother.

"She's okay." The lie tasted bitter on his tongue. Kara Jennings was anything but *okay*. The woman had curves that set him on fire. He'd never gone for short-haired girls before, but her pixie curls framed her face perfectly, offsetting the harshness of her eyes. The light dusting of freckles across her button nose softened her features even more, though she'd probably be pissed to hear it.

Michael snorted. "Yeah. Right. If you have her, and you're not done with this yet, she's more than okay. Look, just have your fun, then get the job done. I can't have this heat on me, it's starting to hurt business. People thinking there's a rat in my crew."

"Yeah. I got it. A few more days, the most." Devin eyed the key in his hand. The post office box was twenty feet away. He could finish everything within a few minutes if he wanted to. But the game was bigger than that, and whatever he found in that box would determine where the next piece was placed.

"Fine. Just get it done." The call clicked off and Devin shoved the phone into his back pocket. Michael wouldn't be persuaded to stay away for long. Just because he didn't give any indication that he knew where he was, and who he was, didn't mean shit.

Throwing open the door to the truck, he decided to focus on the next thing first, then he'd worry about the rest. No one lingered in or around the post office, though for a small town that was pretty normal. He checked the number on the key once more then walked down the aisle of boxes. He moved from the smaller boxes to the larger, until he reached the end of the row at the largest of the boxes available. 4769, there it was.

It wasn't the first time he'd be prying into a private box of a dead man. Too many friends died during his deployments, and someone had to have the honor of clearing out their footlockers. He looked at that post office box in the same way.

Without delay, he slid the key in and turned, half expecting it to resist him. A flick of his wrist and the door opened, and dozens of envelopes came spilling out.

"Hey!" A postal worker with a bad limp hobbled over to him. Devin picked up the envelopes that had fallen to the floor and cradled the bundle in his arms. "You opening up box 4769?"

Devin looked to the open door, the key still nestled in its home, and saw no reason for lying. "Yes, sir. Is there a problem?" Another envelope slipped out, landing at his feet.

"No, no problem." The older man waved two hands in front of himself, as though to say he didn't want any either. "I have a few boxes of stuff in the back I been holding on for that box there." He swept his eyes over Devin. "The guy who owns that box… he said someone might be coming to clear it out one day. Asked me to keep anything that didn't fit separate. We don't normally do that, you see, hold for fifteen days then return, but this fella, well, he made it real hard to say no to him." He graced Devin with a crooked grin, showing off his yellowing teeth. Tommy probably made it really worth his while to bend the rules, and in a small post office such as that, it wouldn't be hard to get a personal favor such as that granted.

After a moment of silence Devin softened his stance. "You think I can get it? I'm clearing this out for now, I don't think there'll be any more mail." Think? Unless Tommy had stuff stashed on a schedule somewhere, there wouldn't be another delivery ever.

"Uh, yeah. Sure. I'll get the dolly, that your truck out there?" He jerked a thumb through the big window.

"Yep. I'll just take these out there for now, and come back for the rest." Devin waited for the old man to limp away toward the back office before gathering as much in his arms as he could and taking it out to the truck. Tommy took too many chances. One box would have been fine to keep everything in; sending so many envelopes brought attention. Unwanted attention. And paying off the postal worker, way to bring in a whole new set of witnesses. Dammit.

By the time the truck was loaded up, three boxes were slid into the bed. Three completely full boxes. He must have been sending envelopes weekly for months. Again, nothing he'd told Tommy had been heeded. Tommy just didn't listen. A family trait, from what the last day showed him.

Devin made sure to slip the worker a heavy tip, and gave him his cell number with instructions to let him know if anyone else tried to get to the box. The old man took the fifty-dollar bill hesitatingly but agreed in the end. He walked away muttering something about city folk, but Devin was already pulling out of the parking lot and headed back to the farmhouse. Hopefully, Kara had been a good girl and hadn't gotten herself into any trouble while he was gone. Though locked in her cage, what could she really get herself into?

•••••••

Basements usually had a mildew quality to them. Kara remembered the basement of her childhood home, before her mother had gotten sick, well after her father had bailed. No matter the season, it was always damp and stinky.

This basement, the one where she found herself locked inside of a cage, didn't have that odor. In fact, it had more of a wildflower scent. Probably from the incense she saw sitting on the nightstand beside the king-sized, four-poster bed. The bed that made her mouth water, and her sore muscles ache to be lying in it. The carpeting she stretched out on in the cage wasn't the worst, at least it was soft, but it was by no means comfortable for sleeping. And not after what she'd endured that morning.

Every muscle ached. Her ass did more than ache, it burned every time she rolled onto her back and the carpeting or the blanket brushed over the raw, taut skin. She didn't need a mirror to know there were bruises. The memory of that strap crossing her bottom sent a shiver through her body. It was a pain like none other she'd ever experienced, and if she was lucky she'd never feel it again. Though considering the past day, she felt less confident about being able to succeed with that feat.

She tried not to think about Devin. It was better she didn't. Her reaction to him, no, her body's insane reaction to him made no sense. No matter what her fantasies had been before, his handling of her shouldn't evoke so much damn arousal. Even when her mind screamed against it, her pussy had moistened, clenched, and wanted him to touch her, to fill her. She'd been reduced to a whore. No. Not a whore, his pet. That's what he called her, that's how he treated her. The leather collar around her neck used to walk her, the cage to keep her in, and the bucket to relieve herself in—he'd taken away her humanity.

It shouldn't matter that his fingers felt so damn good on her flesh. The fire in her ass shouldn't have sent her arousal spiraling out of control when he pushed himself into her. And she sure as fuck shouldn't have come on his command, with his permission. Not one moment since he'd woken her on her couch had she been in control. He'd taken all of it, and when she wouldn't give it to him freely, he just ripped it out of her hands.

He had her tied up, naked, completely vulnerable. One quick slice, one jolted movement of his body and he could have killed her if he wanted to. He could have taken the strap or any other evil implement to her body the moment after she sliced his arm with that screwdriver. But he hadn't. He'd waited. Until he was calm? Until he could figure out what punishment to give? Either way, the man hadn't acted out of rash anger. It was almost as though he were truly delivering a punishment for a crime committed. Not revenge. As heavy and painful as the strokes were, no hatred or disgust came through with them. Only chastisement.

And she'd caved. With his fingers on her, his mouth close to her ear, and his cock shoved so deliciously inside of her, she'd given him what he wanted. He knew about the post office box. Sometime after he delicately carried her back to her cage, he'd left the farmhouse. She'd heard the door shut, the dim sound of the truck coming to life. Were they that close to Eagle?

Footsteps overhead caught her attention. He was back already. They must be close to Eagle, if not *in* Eagle, Michigan. Slowly she pulled herself up from the floor, using the bars to bring her to her feet. Her shoulders still ached from being bound, and the rest of her wasn't holding up much better. She wrapped the blanket around her and tucked in the end to keep it from slipping.

"Dev?" A voice, unlike the one she'd quickly become familiar with, called out. The door to the basement must have been closed, because it was muffled. "Devin, you here?"

Maybe it was a friend, or a neighbor. Yes, a neighbor who would help her get out. She nibbled her lower lip, thinking of what to do. If it wasn't someone who would help her, it could be more dangerous.

The door creaked open at the top of the stairs. "Dev, you down there?" She sucked in her breath, trying to think faster, to make a decision. "Guess not… guess that means this pizza is all mine."

Pizza. Food. Her stomach grumbled at the mere mention. When was the last time she ate? Dinner the night before, or was it before that? "Hey!" She stepped to the door and wrapped her fingers around the bars. "Hey! Down here," she called, leaning her head against the cool bars. *Please. Please let it be a neighbor.*

At first she didn't think he'd heard her, but then the footsteps descended the stairs. The visitor jumped off the last step and landed facing her cage. Slowly, she looked up at him. Black boots, dark blue jeans, thick black leather belt, with a shiny badge dangling from it. A cop!

"You're a cop! A policeman! Help me!" She shook the cage, in her excitement. She didn't take her eyes off the badge. "Please! I've been kidnapped. The crazy man left, but he'll be back soon. Please. Get me out of here."

When he didn't say anything or move, she finished her assessment, finding his face. Fuck.

"The crazy man? Devin?"

"Oh, god," she groaned. Same dark brown eyes. Same thick wavy hair, though not cropped as short as Devin's. Even his nose had the same crooked appearance, though toward the left instead of the right. If he smiled, she was sure she'd see a fucking dimple, too. Other than looking a bit younger, he was the spitting image of Devin.

"Nope, not God, just Trevor. Now, why don't you tell me all about this kidnapping." Then he smiled. Two dimples, one on each cheek. She wanted to throw up, or pass out. Passing out would be better.

"You're a cop. You have to help me. I don't care if you arrest him, just let me go," she pleaded.

"Now, if Devin has you in there, it's probably for a good reason." His cavalier attitude wasn't helping. He acted as though he'd just found her sitting on a park bench.

"What? No. It's not for a good reason. He kidnapped me! Let me out!" By the time she was finished, she was nearing hysterics and screaming the words at him. "He beat me! You have to let me go."

"Oh, well, if he beat you, then I'm sure you're in there for a really good reason… and probably for a good while."

"What the fuck is wrong with you?" she screamed, wishing he'd step closer so she could swing her fist at him.

"Lots of things. I'm hungry for one, and my pizza is upstairs getting cold." He pointed to the stairs that led to the kitchen, to where a hot pizza sat waiting to be devoured. Her stomach rumbled again.

"Oh, my god! You are as crazy as him." She could feel the tears starting to well up. How had she gotten into this mess?

"Now, don't cry." Finally, some concern showed in his voice. "When he gets back we'll get this all straightened out, but I can't let you out because… well, one, I don't have the key and two, Devin put you in there, so Devin has to take you out. You don't want to get more of what you already got, do you?"

"More of what…" Her voice trailed off at the sound of new footsteps upstairs.

"Trevor?" Devin's voice carried down the stairs, taking away her breath and kicking her heart back up a few notches.

She tried to give Trevor another pleading look, but his smile only widened. Sick fuck. "Down here, Dev," he called, crossing his arms over his broad chest. Out of frustration for nothing better to do, she stomped her bare foot on the carpeting.

Devin's feet fell fast on the stairs as he ran down them. His eyes swung first to his brother then to her. They narrowed upon looking at her. She followed his gaze as it left her face and traveled downward to the blanket she had tucked around her body. His jaw clenched, and he shook his head in disappointment.

"So, this little girl here was just telling me that you kidnapped her… and beat her. Is that right?"

Devin's eyes never left her as he answered, "Did she?" He crossed his arms over his chest, as if he didn't already look too much like his brother. Having the two of them fixing their stares on her made the room chilly. Devin was mad; no, she'd seen him mad. This was irritated, but with the potential to get real pissed really quick.

Trevor hadn't been able to free her, but at least his presence might keep Devin from beating her again.

"Why don't we go on upstairs and talk about it." Trevor swiveled on his heels, half turning away from her.

"Sure." Devin nodded and closed the gap between the cage and himself. Instinct kicked in, and she backed away from the door. He wouldn't get a hold of her unless he opened the door, and if he opened it, hopefully Trevor would keep him well behaved. He kept his arms crossed and fixed a solid glare on her, one that made her insides tremble, but even she didn't understand what for. The man worked wonders on her nerves. "What did I say about the blanket, pet?" Still pet, not even peaches, and sure as hell not Kara. Damn him.

Her cheeks burned from the memory of him ripping the blanket from her body earlier, before he took her for her *shower.* Clutching the knot, she chanced a look over his shoulder at Trevor. The man raised an eyebrow, a dark eyebrow in question, or curiosity, it didn't matter. He would be no help. Just like a cop, she thought bitterly.

"Answer me," Devin barked, the fierceness of his eyes back in full force. There would be no softness from him, not with Trevor gone or in the room.

A soft whimper worked its way up her throat, but she managed to choke it back down before it escaped. "That it wasn't for clothing. Only sleeping." Her chin rose, but she doubted her eyes matched the bravado. She'd never been very good at faking her emotions.

"Are you sleeping?"

"No."

"New rule, pet. When you talk to me, you'll address me properly. The correct response right there was 'no, Sir.' Do you understand that rule, pet?" He shook his head. "Never mind. Don't answer, you seemed to understand the rule about the blanket but chose to disregard it. We'll see if you can do better with the new rule. Now, give me the blanket." His hand thrust through the bars of the cage, open and palm facing up.

She shook her head, increased the hold on the blanket and took another step back. "N-no." Trevor was there, looking at her, watching the whole scene but not stopping it.

"No?" Devin's eyebrows shot up and his voice lowered. Who knew a whisper could be so terrifying? "Well, that will just add to what's coming, pet. Now give me the blanket. If I have to come in to get it, I'll bind your arms behind you, to the cage, on your feet. You'll be standing at attention until I return. Not a comfortable position, I assure you."

The man hadn't made a promise so far that he didn't carry through, and she had no reason to expect it happen now. He would make good on his threat. Her body already cried with each movement; being put in such a position would only make her physical pain worse.

Tentatively, she walked over to him, keeping her eyes on his chest. She couldn't meet his eyes, or Trevor's. She didn't want anything from him other than to leave her alone, why couldn't he do that? She yanked the corner of the blanket out of its place and unwrapped her body, exposing her nakedness to both men. The humiliation began to seep into her body, her cheeks flamed, and she clenched her teeth to ward off tears. He had said he liked to see them fall down her face; well, she wouldn't give them to him anymore. She'd hold back. She could do that.

She'd gotten good at keeping her tears at bay when her mother was sick. Not wanting to make her mom feel bad about making her sad, she had learned to clench her teeth, dig her nails into her palm, anything to divert the pain from her chest to a physical pain. Physical being easier to deal with. But she'd never perfected keeping it from her eyes; her mother always knew.

No one was there now though. It was just her, like always. All those years trying to keep Tommy out of trouble, keep him from doing the shit he did anyway had worn her down, making taking care of herself harder and harder to do. But walls, she could still put up the walls when needed. And at that moment, it was needed.

She laid the blanket over his arm and crossed her arms over her own chest, backing up again.

Wordlessly, he pulled it through the bars and went about folding it. Taking his time, he placed corner to corner, pressing down the crease and repeating the action until the blanket sat in his hand, the perfect square. "Behave yourself, start obeying, and you'll earn this back." He tucked it under his arm. "How is your ass?"

"Fine." She took another step back.

His lips, those warm, dominating lips, parted slightly, like he was going to say something, then snapped shut. Maybe he did have some manners after all. "I'll check when I get back down. We have a few things to talk about, pet, and it will be in your best interest to behave from this point on."

"Can I use the washroom? Please." She tried to sweeten her voice, but found the contempt rising too high in her throat to be successful.

He shook his head with a little laugh. "You think because my brother's here, I'll relent? Not going to happen. You'll earn that privilege back with obedience. Not before. The bucket's there if you need." With that said he turned away and walked up the stairs.

"Your pizza's getting cold," she snapped at Trevor when he remained still staring at her. Her hands were over her breasts, but her pubic hair was exposed.

"I'd watch your tone. I don't think your owner would like you speaking to me that way." The corner of his mouth lifted in what she normally would have considered a devastatingly handsome grin, were it not being given by the monster's brother, but he was.

"He's not my owner. I'm not a fucking pet. I'm a kidnapped woman, who you are completely ignoring. Your brother is a kidnapper. What kind of cop are you? Do you have no fucking morals at all?"

A shadow crossed his face, the smile faded away, and his hands dropped to his sides. "Careful, little girl. You have no idea what bear you're poking. If I were you, I'd do exactly what Devin says. Whatever punishment he's given you so far isn't nearly as bad as it could be. You'd do well to remember that. Everything can always get worse than it is right now."

Before she could find a retort he was gone, heading up the stairs to join his brother for a nice pizza lunch. Her mouth watered at the very thought of the melted cheese, spicy tomato sauce. She slapped the bars of the cage and screamed into the empty space. Nothing coherent, just a scream to release the pressure building in her chest before it exploded. Because no matter what happened to her in that basement, she was not going to let Devin break her. She was her own person. She belonged to no one. And if that meant she'd be completely on her own, so be it. What did she really have to go back to Chicago for anyway? Her mom was gone, Tommy was gone; other than Julie at work, she had no friends and being a medical receptionist wasn't exactly reaching her potential. So no, he wouldn't break her.

She'd never allow it.

CHAPTER EIGHT

"So. Your pet." Trevor snagged a piece of cheese pizza from the box sitting in the kitchen table, grease seeping through the cardboard and onto the table, no doubt. No one made pizza right, not outside the city anyway.

"Yeah." Devin shut the basement door. She'd be listening in on them, and he couldn't have her getting too much information.

The kitchen chair scraped against the ceramic tiles of the floor as Devin sat with his brother, dropping the blanket on one of the empty chairs.

"What's going on here, Dev? Why is she locked up?"

Devin pulled up his left sleeve and showed him the nearly scabbed scratch on his arm.

Trevor laughed and took another bite of his pizza. "That little thing did that? How'd she get a knife?"

"Not a knife. A fucking screwdriver. I left the toolbox in the bathroom."

"You're slipping in your old age, Dev. What's she doing here anyway, who is she?"

"Kara Jennings." Devin ignored the scowl that replaced the taunting smirk on Trevor's expression and reached for a piece of pizza.

"Tommy Jennings' little sister? What the fuck is she doing here?" Trevor dropped his half-eaten slice back into the box and scooted away from the table, wiping his hands on his jeans.

"There's paper towels over there." Devin pointed to the counter. "She's here for safekeeping. Till I get what I need."

"Then what?" Trevor reached behind him, tilting the chair back onto its back legs to grab the roll of paper towels on the counter.

"Depends," Devin shrugged, stuffing the last bite of pizza into his mouth. "I got groceries in the truck. I'm gonna get them, then you can tell me what brings you here anyway. I never told you I'd be up here this week."

Trevor didn't get a chance to answer him as Devin walked out to the truck to bring in the bags of food. What little stuff his contractors had left would run out in a day or so, and they'd need more. Leaving her alone in the house left him concerned, so the less he needed to do that, the better.

Once the groceries were all in the house, and the boxes from the post office were stacked on the table as well, he glanced over at Trevor, who was piling pizza on a plate. "What are you doing?"

"Didn't you hear her stomach growl when we were down there? The girl's starved."

"I left her some toast this morning, she's fine… I'll feed her later. Once you've gone." He tossed a box of cereal at Trevor, who caught it and placed it on the counter. "Don't go getting soft on me."

"Why do you have her?"

"I thought we agreed that until this was over with Michael Cardone, you weren't going to go asking questions. I can't tell you and you don't want to know, so leave it be." Devin gave a pointed stare at the badge hanging from Trevor's hip. "What are you up here for anyway? That badge doesn't mean anything up here."

Trevor tucked the last bit of canned soup into the

cabinet and leaned against the counter.

"Missing person's case. A spoiled brat of a girl got a bee up her ass and hightailed it out of Chicago. I was just going to make a pit stop, eat and take a quick nap, but I saw the tracks from your truck, and the front door was open. Didn't expect to find that beauty down there though. That was a surprise."

"Leave her be, don't go down there anymore. She needs some rest; the afternoon is going to be hard for her."

Trevor studied Devin for a long moment. "What's going on, really."

"Leave it be, Trevor."

"You can't keep her, you know. After whatever you're going to do, you can't keep her."

"I said leave it be." Devin took the plate with pizza on it and put it in the fridge. Keeping her wasn't a question. After everything worked its way out, she wouldn't want to keep him anyway. Not after the things he'd done, the person he'd had to become, the person he wouldn't stop being. She brought out an animal instinct in him, to possess and devour.

"She thinks you're a kidnapper, which is pretty easy to see how she assumed that."

"She said that, did she?"

"I'm guessing you haven't told her then?" The accusation was there, but Devin wasn't going to play into it.

"No need. Not yet."

"You don't think she deserves to know? "

"Dammit. I think it's been too long since I kicked your ass. I said leave it be." She was on a completely need-to-know basis, and at the moment the less he told her, the better for them both.

Trevor sighed and looked at the closed door. "You really beat her?"

Devin shot him a disgruntled look. The exasperation was building to an intolerable level. "A strapping, and barely what she deserved. You know how stubborn Ma was?

Nothing compared to that woman down there." He jerked his chin in the direction of the door. "Thinks the whole fucking world resides under her care. She actually believes that it's her fault Tommy got killed. She didn't save him, didn't stop him from being the bastard that he was."

Trevor only shook his head. "You're getting too close." When Devin started to respond he pointed to the boxes on the table. "What are those?"

"Nothing you need to worry about."

"The tapes?"

"Really, you are a pain in my ass."

Trevor shot him a grin. "Want me to help sort?"

"Don't you have a damsel in distress to fucking save?" Devin scratched behind his ear. His brother normally knew when to back off, when to stay out of his work; it had to be Kara keeping him so interested.

"She'll keep." The smile slipped, but Trevor recovered quickly. "She's not going anywhere. I know where she is."

"How is she a missing person's case if you know where she is? How old is she?"

"Mid-twenties, I think. Her dad sits on some committee back home. Her running off has pissed him off something fierce. Not enough to go after her himself, mind you, but enough to call in a favor at the department." Trevor had worked missing persons for nearly five years already. "Need to keep it quiet though, so I got picked. Yay me." He waved two hands in the air. "Can't wait to meet her, she sounds like a gem."

Devin laughed. "Well, get what you need, then get out of here. I need to finish up, and I can't do that with you here. She thinks you're gonna save her, and she can't be thinking anyone's coming to save her." He pulled out the first envelope in one of the boxes and tore into it. "Because no one is."

• • • • • • •

The more Kara tried to hear what was going on upstairs, the louder her stomach growled. The buttered toast he'd left her for her earlier hadn't been enough to hold her over for very long. The least he could do was feed her, after beating on her and… well, fucking her. She couldn't call what he did rape, which only compounded her embarrassment and shame.

After going over the whole thing in her mind again and again, she knew she hadn't told him no, hadn't asked him to stop once his fingers were on her. Just thinking about his cock inside of her made her want it to happen again. But it wouldn't. It couldn't. She could chalk up the first time to not having had a man's physical attention in some time. A long time, really, but she couldn't use that excuse if she let it happen a second time. No matter how much what he did aroused her, and why the hell did it, she wanted to know.

She was no stranger to corporal punishment play, at least in theory, but what he did wasn't a little hand spanking over her naughty bottom. What he did, it was real. And it hurt. Her body shouldn't have reacted the way it had, her mind sure as hell should have shut down the whole damn thing. Instead she'd found herself actually wishing he'd fuck her harder. Taking her breath away, literally with the damn collar, should not have made her body clench with such desire.

The door finally opened, and she backed up to the other end of the cage, sinking down to sit with her knees pressed firmly against her chest. Without the blanket she had nothing to help shield her from his view, or protect her from the chill in the room.

Only one set of footsteps signaled his approach. Did his brother stay upstairs or was he gone? Not that he would have been much help anyway.

"Trevor said to tell you bye." His deep voice resonated in the cell. "Said to behave." He gave a little chuckle as he slid the key into the lock. "Though, I'm not sure which of us that was intended for." The right corner of his mouth ticked up in a half grin, making him look almost playful. She looked away. "I want to check your ass; stand up and turn around."

Remembering her new decision, finding some resolve hidden inside of her, she shook her head. "No." But she hadn't looked at him yet. Didn't know how he reacted, but he didn't move, so she had some hope.

"New rule, though I'm sure we already covered this with the whole obey rule, but you don't get to say no to me. Not when I'm giving you an order. Now. Stand up and turn around."

Turning to face him, she swallowed hard—those dark eyes of his were on her, narrowed and looking sterner than before. "N-no." She wrapped her arms around her knees and tugged them tighter to her chest.

His jaw clenched, but he didn't say anything else. Instead he left the cage and walked over to the wall, the one with all the dreaded implements hanging. He tapped his chin, as though the deliberating was really taking a toll on him, then plucked a thick leather strap from its hook. It looked a little less deadly than the razor strap, and she let out a breath.

"You've got some coming to you already, so I would think real hard before you disobey me again. Get up and turn around. If you follow orders now, you'll only get what you've got coming, a belting to your ass. If you disobey again, you'll take a fucking as well."

"You'd force me again?" she shot at him, wishing she could hurt him.

"Force?" He tilted his head. "There was no force, but you think it would be easier if there had been. I see the shame in your eyes, pet. There shouldn't be, it was good, what we did out there. You took your whipping well, and you had a good fuck to cleanse your system. No shame there to be had. But if you don't listen, if you keep resisting the rules here, you'll take a hard fucking—used like a little whore, like my pet." All levity left his expression and his jaw tightened. "Get. Up. And. Turn around."

"My ass is fine," she whispered, feeling the tears already burning her eyes. "I'm fine."

"That was your chance." He walked over to her and gripped her arm, yanking her to her feet. His nose touched hers, the smell of his pizza lunch washed over her. "Turn around." Before she could move to obey, he twisted her and pressed her against the bars. "Hold the bars," he ordered, a little less fire in his voice.

She wrapped her fingers around the bars. Fingers were on her back, trailing downward toward her ass. He shifted behind her. His hands ran over the tender areas of her ass. "No bruising, that's good. Still sore, I bet, will be hell of a lot more in a minute, but looks good." He patted her ass softly. She breathed a sigh, thinking he was finished.

She should have known better. His hands were back on her, pulling her ass cheeks apart, wide. The stretch hurt, and she moved up onto her tiptoes. "Settle down. I'm just looking." His thumb trailed over her tight pucker, a light touch that made her body react the same as if he'd touched her clit. She heard a popping sound from behind her, then felt his wet thumb back on her, pushing inward on her hole.

"Devin!" She tried to clench her ass cheeks together, but he replaced his grip on her, keeping her spread wide for his eyes.

"Relax. It wouldn't hurt so much if you'd relax."

Even if she wanted to, the idea of what was to come made her body tense too much. He sighed heavily then gave one hard push, and his thumb was inside. His thumb was inside her ass. It was too much. She started to wiggle, but he put a hard hand on her back, pressing her to the bars. "You ever been fucked here, pet?" He began to move his thumb in and out of her. Slow and methodical. The intense burn she felt on the initial thrust faded into a warmth that spread through her, to her clit.

"No." Hot tears rolled down her cheeks.

"Hmm." He pulled his thumb out and gave her ass a harsh slap. "Let's get this over with. You need to eat something, but first you need to learn your lesson. Keep holding the bars, don't let go, and don't try to get away. You're getting ten lashes, pet. Ten. And when I'm done, you're going to thank me, and offer your pussy up for your fucking. Got it?"

What choice did she really have? His thick, masculine body blocked the cell door, and even if she managed to get past him, there was the little matter of the stairs, the front hall, the door, then a vast sea of nothingness for miles around that she could recall. And the small matter of her lack of clothing.

She put her mind to hating him. Her ass clenched in anticipation of the thick leather he held in his hand. He rubbed her bottom, making her twitch from the unexpected gentleness of his touch. A soft hand over one cheek, then moving to the second. "So soon after your strapping." He sounded almost regretful, as though maybe he didn't want to go through with it. He kept rubbing, and she turned her focus to his breathing. Calm. Not ragged and heavy like her own, but damn near tranquil. Just when she thought maybe he'd stopped being upset, had forgiven her misstep, he pulled his hand away and stepped back.

"Ten."

Her fingers tightened, her ass clenched harder. He hadn't forgiven; he wasn't going to relent. He'd give her ten, because he said ten, and all she could do was take it. New tears sprang to her eyes, she felt her shoulders shake and realized she was crying. For what was going to happen or for what had already transpired, didn't matter. He was breaking her.

The first lash landed, sending her mind reeling into the present, forgetting coherent thought as the leather belt came down a second time. She barely had time to catch her breath before the third and fourth landed. Up on tiptoe she clenched hard, screamed out from the electric burn he put into her ass with the fifth.

"Be a good girl now, soften those cheeks. Clenching

won't help you, and it only makes me go harder. Soften up, and put your heels down."

A sob broke from her chest as she complied, obeying him to get into proper position so he could continue punishing her. More fat tears dripped from her chin and landed on her naked breasts, but she didn't bother trying to wipe them away, too many were ready to spill next. There would be no point.

"Good girl." He ran a hand over her newly heated ass. "Five more."

Her sobbing took on a new power. She couldn't stand five more, she ached, she was scared, she was tired. So tired. His hand left her ass and touched her head, running his fingers through her short curls. There would be no stay of execution, he had decreed it and so it would be done. Nothing was going to stop him now, not her cries or her screams. Not even the small amount of tenderness he showed her at that moment. It wasn't over, he was giving her a chance to take a breath and get back into position.

"Right." He patted her head, like he would any other pet and stepped back into his position.

The belt crashed down, harder than before, and lower. Right across the curve of her ass. Another lash, just above that one. He was a man on a mission, with a job to do. The last three lashes came fast and hard. Harder than she could comprehend.

By the time the last of the ten were delivered, her throat burned almost as much as her backside. The raw pain resonated through her entire body. Leaning against the bars, she let herself cry, sniffling and mentally chiding herself for letting him see how much he'd gotten into her head.

His body blanketed her, pressing her into the bars of the cage. Her cage. Warm hands ran down her sides until he reached her hips. Traveling forward, she closed her eyes against his fingers making their way to what she knew would be her wet desires.

"You took your whipping well, pet." His jeans grazed

her raw ass and she winced, sucking in air and crying even more into the crook of her arm. One finger found her clit. "So wet," he whispered into her ear. "So damn wet for me, even when it hurts. Even when you've been punished for being so naughty, so damn naughty, your pussy knows what to do. For me. Because this pussy," he cupped her mound and pulled back, pressing her ass further against his jeans, "this pussy is mine, now, pet. All mine."

"Until you decide to dump me or hand me over." She whispered the statement as though it were true enough to carve in stone.

"Not going to happen," he promised. "You're mine until I say otherwise." He thrust two fingers inside of her, filling her and easing the ache he'd created there. She hated him. For kidnapping her, spanking her, binding her, gagging her, and for making her fill with shame and horror at her own feelings. "No, don't pull away, don't try to escape. You love this, you crave it."

She didn't respond. He'd know if she lied; hell, her pussy was clenching around his fingers, dripping her arousal down his hand.

His free hand went behind her, she felt and heard the buckle of belt being undone, the zipper of his jeans being yanked down. Then the head of his cock pressed against her ass. Raw as it was, feeling him hard for her, feeling the strength of just his cock pushing at her turned the hurt into something new, something almost tangible.

"Keep your hands on the bars, pet. Arch your back a bit, offer up your pussy."

The question of what would happen if she said no tingled the tip of her tongue, but she knew. Telling him no wasn't allowed, but if she really didn't want him, if she meant her refusal, she knew he'd stop. He was turning out to be many things, but he wasn't the evil villain she'd thought. Besides, did she even want him to stop at that moment? Her punishment wasn't over. The whipping had given her a physical reminder of who was in charge, who was the owner. The fucking would show her how much he controlled her mental state. The pet answering to his call.

Her feet wiggled apart, spreading her legs further, and she pushed her ass toward him, sucking in her breath as her raw ass rubbed against him again. He slipped his hand away from her pussy and grabbed her ass. Not hard like she half expected, but with some gentleness. Her skin was too alive with pain for it to feel good, but she wasn't itching to jump away from him either. "There's a welt, an ugly one right here." He put a little more pressure on the spot, and ran his finger along it. She hissed but still didn't try to move away. "I don't like punishing you like that, pet."

Considering his cock was stiff as steel and ready to plunge into her, she didn't quite believe him.

Her cheeks were spread wide, and for a moment she feared he'd plunge into her ass. Bracing herself for such an action, she gripped the bars harder, holding her breath and waiting. The head of his cock ran over her puckered hole, then moved lower to her pussy. The smooth head of his dick pressed into her aching wet entrance, and like the whore he was making her to be, she arched her back even more to give him better access.

"That's a good girl." He let go of her ass cheeks, gripping her hips instead. His nails bit into her skin, but compared to the fire still burning bright on her ass cheeks, it wasn't noteworthy. With one hard thrust, he plunged into her, his balls bounced against her clit. Just the light brush sent shocks of arousal throughout her body, and for a moment, she wished he'd touch her again. That he wouldn't just take her like some pet used for his pleasure, some toy stored in his playroom, but would fulfill her, give her the pleasure he had given her earlier.

Not this time. The sensations he gave were different, more demanding. He was sending a message, teaching a lesson. His finger dug into her harder, his thrusts became more urgent, more powerful. She gasped as he filled her over and over again, the newest ache starting lower in her stomach. She tried to grip the bars harder, to keep from moving but he fucked her harder still. Her breath picked up the pace until she was panting like a dog.

Like a fucking pet. Did the man know any other way of driving his point home then treating her so wickedly? So boldly?

One hand dove into her hair, yanking her head back until his lips could reach her ear. He kissed the small tender spot right below, right where the nerve endings connected to her clit. If such a connection was real, she didn't know for sure, but her body told her it was. "Take your fucking, pet. That's a good girl." He nipped her earlobe, sending more urgency into her own body. She moved against him, wishing she held the courage to release the bar and slip her hand between her legs. Just a little release, something to make the moment less of a torment. Too much pleasure, without any hope of relief.

Her heels left the floor again as he plunged deeper still, harder than she thought he could in their position. Her hair strained against her scalp, a single tear shed from her eye, rolling down her temple as she looked up at the top of the cage.

"Fuck!" he growled and thrust hard, then gripped her hips with both hands as he plunged once more and stilled behind her, letting his come spurt inside of her.

His heavy breathing was the only sound in the room. She closed her eyes, silently letting the rest of her tears fall. She didn't even know why she was crying anymore. For the orgasm he denied her?

After a few long moments, he slid out of her body, tucking his cock away and zipping his pants. He patted her ass, reminding her of the whipping he'd given her, as though the heat had resolved at all in the last few minutes that his pelvis was pounding against her, renewing the flame.

"You need some rest. I'll make you something to eat." He left the cell for a moment to retrieve a pillow from the bed, bringing it back and dropping it on top the other, much older and flatter one she had been using. No blanket though. No, that was another punishment. Another lesson in obedience. She supposed she should be grateful for the small gift. Perhaps she'd be able to use a real toilet.

"Thank you," she whispered, almost meaning it. The pillow had been a small gesture; it deserved a small gesture in return.

She stepped around him, careful not to let her body brush against him. With her head ducked down, she wiped her cheeks and slid to the floor. Even with turning on her side, she felt the harshness of the carpet against her ass. A few lashes had wrapped her hip, enough to make lying on either side uncomfortable. He probably wanted it that way, making her feel the belting every time she moved. The skin on her ass felt so stretched, so abused, she wanted to lie on her stomach, but she'd never been a stomach sleeper.

When he squatted down in front of her, she recoiled into herself, sliding back until the cool metal of the bars touched her hot ass. The momentary lapse of heat quickly turned into discomfort at having her backside touched.

"Shhh." With a gentle touch, he swiped the hair away from her face, tucking it behind her ear. When her eyes met his, there was kindness, concern lingering there. It didn't last. It flashed away, leaving a hard gaze in its place. "The punishment's over, pet." She hated that name. That fucking name. She'd rather he'd go back to calling her peaches. "I want you to rest, try to get some sleep while I fix some lunch. You haven't eaten in too long. I'll get you some water, too."

With as flat of a voice as she could muster she asked the question tearing her insides apart. "Why did they kill Tommy? Why like that? Are they going to do the same to me?"

He yanked his hand back, as though her skin burned him, but recovered quickly and went back to stroking her face. After a moment of purposeful silence, he seemed to have made a decision. "I'm sorry about Tommy. I tried to protect him, to save him, but he didn't listen. Much like his little sister, he felt he knew better—but he didn't. Just like his little sister."

The small part in her that was supposed to start blaring a warning signal when someone lied or tried to manipulate her didn't go off. Instead, an incredible sense of relief ran through her body, soothing aching muscles and tense nerves. "Tommy never listened to anyone. I tried." A sob stopped her from continuing, but she shoved it back down. "I tried to make him listen, to make him stop. If I had been better, if I hadn't been so young, so unable to help him, he never would have started up with those people."

A dark shadow crossed his features, his jaw clenched again. She'd said something to piss him off, but what?

"Tommy was ten years older than you; the responsibility was on him to take care of you, not the other way around. And there are plenty of ways he could've done that without putting himself at risk—you at risk, for a quick buck." Hadn't she said the same thing to Tommy, millions of times?

"You knew him, then. I mean, I know you did, but well?"

"I knew him enough." The backs of his fingers ran down her cheek before his fingertips trailed over her lips. "I couldn't protect him, but I will protect you."

"Is that what all this is? You protecting me?" She pulled her head back, away from his touch. Her ass would beg to differ, as well as every other sore muscle in her body. "I saw what they did to him," she whispered, not looking at him anymore. She didn't want to see the flicker of compassion only to see it fly away a moment later once he regained his composure.

"You shouldn't have—"

"My fault, remember? The least I could do was see what happened, witness it for myself. Why should I get the comfort of not knowing how tortured he was because I failed him?" She hadn't meant to snap, to sound so harsh; it could get her another lashing, and her ass couldn't take any more.

He didn't react to her micro-burst of anger. "Get some sleep. I'll wake you when lunch is ready. If you are a good girl, I'll let you come upstairs for lunch."

Upstairs. Where real light was. Furniture he would let her use, and maybe the bathroom.

Not trusting herself to open her mouth, and feeling the heaviness of her eyelids, she nodded and nestled into the comfort of the added pillow. Something so fine and plush as that had never been a part of her household; she would treasure the moments with it. Sure that he would take it back the moment she said something that displeased him.

She listened to the cell door shut and lock, and his footsteps fade away up the stairs. The upstairs door didn't close. He'd leave it open to hear if she called for him.

She wouldn't call for him; she needed to get strong so she could figure out how to get away from him.

And all of the tormenting wonderful feelings he seemed to be able to kindle to life within her.

He was dangerous. And she was done with dangerous.

CHAPTER NINE

She blamed herself, he already knew that, but to hear her say the words. To feel the vibrations in her body as the pain of her self-accusation settled inside, dragged out a rage inside of him he'd locked up a long time ago.

Tommy was supposed to take care of her, not the other way around. She had been twelve when her mother died. Twelve! She needed a brother who would pay rent, put dinner on the table, and made sure her ass studied. Not go around slinging drugs, collecting back rents, and any other bullshit thing Michael Cardone asked him to do. The risk to himself and to her was too great.

She blamed herself for being too young to help.

Fuck.

Trevor was right; he was getting too close. Everything was getting too crowded. Trevor had sent him at least half a dozen texts since he left, asking about her. The bastard had taken a liking to her in the five minutes he'd spent with her. Trevor didn't understand what ran through her head, what tore at her and made her tick. But he did. Devin knew. He could feel her when she was near. The energy rolling off her body when he was around. It shifted, the moment he entered her cage, her eyes may have widened in fear—and fuck him for liking that, but he did—but her pupils spread across her dark eyes, too. She hated that he whipped her, but she hated that she liked it even more.

A shuffling sound from downstairs let him know she'd woken up. The handle of the bucket clanking against the rim suggested she was using it. He waited with the bowl of warm rice and vegetables on the table until he was sure she'd be finished. He wanted some modicum of cooperation from her to get her to eat, so he let her have the privacy she wanted before going down to fetch her.

Without a blanket to cover her body, she stood near the cell door with goose pimples running rampant over her body. Even after the time in the cell, the spankings, the fighting, she still looked hotter than his body could ignore. Her arms were folded over her stomach, which only lifted her tits higher and made him want to tweak the hardened nubs.

Keeping his eyes on her, he unlocked the cage and stood in the doorway. "I'm going to take you upstairs and I expect you to eat all of your lunch. I'm not going to use your leash, because I'm giving you this chance. A chance to earn back some of your privileges. Do you understand me, pet?"

"Y-yes?"

He raised an eyebrow.

She visibly fought an eye-roll but answered correctly. "Yes, Sir." Her tone lacked any actual sincerity, but it would do. For now.

"Good. Come." He snapped his fingers and pointed to the stairs. The idea of making her crawl all the way up made his cock twitch in his pants. He'd already fucked her twice that day, and just the mental image of seeing her red, welted ass swaying in front of him while she crawled for him make him ready to do it again.

In the end, he settled for having her walk behind him. She may look docile after having taken a short nap, but he hadn't taken a nap and he wasn't up to chasing her down again.

He heard her intake of breath with the first step up the stairs. Her ass would be sore for a few days after the belting he'd given her. Maybe she'd manage to take note of a few things now that sitting would be a little more difficult than before.

But then again, sitting wasn't what he had in mind when it came to get her anyway.

Once up in the kitchen, he moved to the chair at the table with the bowl of food. She shot her hand out in front of him and grasped the chair beside it, scraping the legs against the flooring as she pulled it from the table.

"Whoa. What are you doing?" he asked, covering her hands with his own.

She gave him a wary glance. "Sitting down."

It was almost too hard to take away the hope simmering in her eyes. Almost.

"You haven't earned any privileges yet. You'll kneel here, at my feet, like a good pet."

Her dark, narrowed eyes followed his pointed finger to the spot on the floor, next to his chair. To her credit, she didn't yank her hand away or shout at him. Though he could see several retorts forming in that brain of hers. Even if he wanted her complete obedience, he still appreciated her quick wit. Life would just be too boring if she behaved robotically.

"I know you're still pissed, but I've already apologized and went through the humiliating punishments. Can't you just let me eat like a person?" The pleading was there, but so was the underlying demand. She still expected things to go her way.

"I'm not pissed anymore." He shook his head. "You took your punishments, but you still haven't earned the privileges back. So, you'll kneel beside me, and I'll feed you." He let go of her hand, letting her take a moment to mull it over, and sure that she would cave. The woman had to be starving, and thirsty. The only way those two needs were being met was at his discretion, in his way. Because her way, her all in charge, 'I don't need anyone' way didn't work—not for her, and sure as fuck not for him.

She eyed the bowl of rice and vegetables, all but drooling from her mouth. The image that flashed in his mind of that exact thing taking place excited him. The beast was getting harder to contain, the more he imagined things like that.

Making up her mind took another long pause, but she shot him a look that suggested he go fuck himself, and stepped around him. He turned to watch as she gracefully sank to her knees beside his chair, leaning back on her heels, then quickly leaning back up. Her ass would bruise; two serious spankings in one day would do that.

Once she seemed settled and her eyes were locked on the bowl, he took his seat, facing forward, not looking down at her. Taking a spoonful of the food, he shoveled it into his mouth. He wasn't all that hungry, the pizza he shared with Trevor earlier had tided him over, but she didn't know that. It wasn't the point. After another bite, and feeling her tense up beside him, he scooped some of the rice and sautéed bell pepper into his right hand and held it out to her, just below her mouth.

"What are you doing?" She eyed his hand as though he were offering her poison.

"Feeding you. Take it." He lifted it up to her mouth.

She shoved his hand away, knocking the rice to the floor along with the peppers. He tsked his tongue. "Shit." She lowered her head. At least she was starting to realize when she fucked up; now if she could just do it before she got herself into trouble, they'd be making progress.

He left her kneeling there, her head hung and her eyes staring at the clump of rice on the floor. A part of him was going to enjoy the next few minutes, another part tried to get that part of him to shut up.

Retrieving the special bowl from the farthest cabinet in the kitchen, he returned to her. He scraped the rest of the lunch into it and placed it in front of her on the floor. He could all but hear the muscles in her body clench at what he'd put in front of her.

A shiny new dog bowl, complete with the word *PET* inscribed with black ink on the side. "No, no." He swatted her hand away when she reached for the rice. "That's not how pets eat. I tried the polite way, but you didn't want it, so this is how it is. For now, at least."

"How am I supposed to—" Her face blanched momentarily at the realization. "Like a dog?" The whispered sentence didn't really require a response; she'd gotten the gist of the exercise.

He pushed the bowl a little further away from her with his foot and came down to his haunches. Lifting her chin up with his hand and remaining silent until her eyes settled on his, he tried to give her a comforting grin. "It will be easier if you get on all fours, pet. Put your ass up in the air for me, and eat your lunch. When you're done we'll talk." His thumb caught another tear that slipped down her cheek, and he placed a warm kiss to her lips. A quick, soft kiss. "I'm not angry with you. I'm teaching you."

"Teaching me what exactly? How to be humiliated every second of the day?" She shot the question out at him, but it lacked heat.

"No. You need to learn it's okay to depend on someone. You need protecting, that's my job. You need to let me protect you, that's your job. Nothing we've done, or will do, is outside the very things you crave. If you would stop fighting yourself, and me, you'd see that."

She ignored the second part of his explanation. "If I don't want your protection?" Did she realize that her face was leaning into his hand? He doubted it.

"Sometimes what we want and what we need aren't the same thing." He gave a pointed look at the bowl in front of her. "You can do this. You can show me how good you can behave, then I can start giving things back to you. Like a hot bath? You'd like that, I bet. Your muscles must be stiff. Eat your lunch like a good girl, drink your water." He patted her cheek then stood up before she could even respond.

While he filled a second bowl with water for her, he heard the cuffs on her wrists jingle. When he turned back to her from the sink, he wasn't all that surprised to see her already in place. Leaning down on her forearms, her ass—still a warm red with a few ugly welts and one light bruise—was high in the air. He could see her pussy perfectly from where he stood, the plump lips already glistening from her arousal. Damn, the woman got off on objectification, but just didn't know it, or refused to admit it; either way, they were both having their needs met at that moment, even if she was less aware than him about it.

He knelt down to place the water bowl beside the rice. She didn't look up to see him, but that didn't stop him from enjoying the view. Her lips curled around a clump of rice, and she chewed quickly before swallowing it, then diving in for more. "Drink, too; you don't want to get dehydrated."

She didn't respond, and he didn't force her. Giving her a little space, he went over to the box sitting on the table still. He'd gone through all of the envelopes while she rested. A small pile of tapes and several stacks of cash were in the box. Once she was finished with her lunch, he'd get some answers.

He pulled the chair out from the table and took a seat, crossing his arms over his chest while he watched his captive enjoy her lunch. The stiff cock in his pants would have to go unpleasured for a little while at least; he needed to start making progress or they'd both be in more danger than he could control from all sides.

Once she finished the rice, she moved over to the water bowl. Her hair covered most of her face and she kept trying to tuck it behind her ear, or flip it back, but still it fell forward into the bowl. Deciding he'd been a bystander long enough, he moved back to her side.

She didn't flinch when he touched her, placing a gentle hand on her upturned ass. He pulled her hair back and held it in one fist, letting her drink without it bothering her. He watched her pink tongue lap up the water, a soft blush settled on her cheeks. She loved it, and hated herself for it, too. He wondered how many times she had fantasized about such things, never expecting it to really happen.

"That's my good girl," he whispered softly, running his left hand down her back, stroking her softly as she drank. He heard the moan, a slight sound that she probably hadn't meant to let loose, but he'd heard it. He continued to hold her hair back and pet her until she was finished drinking.

He let her hair go, but continued to rub her back when she went back to kneeling. "Your backside is still red, and you'll have a bruise or two." He tucked the hair on the right side of her face behind her ear. She looked up at him, her lips still damp from the water bowl, one piece of rice stuck to her chin. He picked it off and put it back in the bowl. "Would you like to use the toilet, peaches?"

Her eyes lit up at the question. "Okay then. One sec." He stood up and went to the pantry, plucking the short chained lead from the hook he went back to her. "Let's go." He clipped the lead to her collar and pointed for her to move down the hall. He shook his head when she started to stand up. With a grimace, but no backtalk, she sank back to her knees and began to crawl. He stepped over her, to lead her down the hall to the full bath.

He didn't have to, but he walked her all the way into the room to the toilet. He didn't unleash her, but let go of the handle. "Go and then come back out to the hall."

She nodded that she'd heard him, but he doubted she understood much of anything anymore.

Hell, none of this made sense to him either. He left her by herself and stepped outside, only closing the door halfway, but giving her more privacy she'd had since the day before.

• • • • • • •

Kara finished washing her hands and took a moment to look herself in the mirror. Her hair had seen better days.

Whatever soap he'd put in it that morning may have cleaned it, but made her curls uncontrollable and frizzy. At least her eyes weren't red anymore; she was tired of crying. It made her look weak, and she wasn't. A slut and a whore, but not weak.

Eating her lunch out of the pet bowls should have destroyed her. It may have, had Devin not been the one ordering it. He hadn't just sat there and watched her humiliation; he joined in with her. He'd held her hair back when it kept getting into the water bowl, and had stroked her. Petted her like the pet she was to him, yes, but it was a comforting gesture, not a cruel, insulting one. He'd walked her through the moment and brought her out unscathed on the other side.

He said they would talk after lunch. Did he have questions or did he have answers? He seemed to know more about Tommy than she did. Knowing how much she hated what he did, Tommy never gave her details. He just called it work and said he had a shift. Whatever that meant. If he was on shift somewhere, there'd be a paycheck. Not just an envelope of cash on his kitchen table, or in his nightstand. Not just a little envelope either. At one point she'd gotten to his apartment before him, they were meeting up for dinner, and she'd seen a wad of cash on the counter that totaled nearly ten grand. When she'd asked him about it, he swept it into a drawer and told her not to worry. He'd shoved some money at her again that night, but she refused it. The same way she always did. Her hope had always been that if he saw she wouldn't take the money, wouldn't take what he was providing, maybe he'd stop doing whatever he was doing. Maybe he'd get a job, learn a trade, do something that didn't leave her sleepless on nights she knew he was *on shift*.

Kara shook away thoughts of Tommy. Nothing she tried ever worked, and he was dead because of it.

She started to step toward the door but stopped herself. He'd let her use the bathroom because she'd not argued about the bowls. She'd gone along with him. Better to keep on that route. Maybe that shower he mentioned would be the next reward.

Sinking back to the floor, she crawled to the door, pulling it open. He didn't say a word, just put his hand out toward her. Taking a guess at what he wanted, she handed him the leash. "Good girl." He patted her head and started walking back down the hall to the kitchen.

Good girl. How many times had she fantasized about hearing those words? She'd always imagined a warmth erupting in her chest when she heard them, but it was different in real life. Though that probably had more to do with who was saying them than the actual words. The warmth was there, but it wasn't what she expected. She figured she should feel some shame, him being a kidnapping bastard and all, but instead the warmth warped into a sense of something else. Pride? Fuck, she was crazier than she thought, and it would only get worse the longer she stayed with him.

He walked her back to the bowls and unlatched the leash. He snatched up the rice bowl, not that there was much rice left. She'd been famished, and completely pigged out on the rice and vegetables. The pizza would have been good, but she doubted either of the brothers thought to save her a piece. Besides, they weren't in Chicago, it probably wasn't all that good anyway. *Keep lying to yourself, Kara!*

She heard the bowl being rinsed off and put in the sink, but didn't look at him. What if he had a pleased smile on his face? Would she grin back like the idiot she was becoming? Better not to tempt herself. Distance, she needed distance.

He sat back down and motioned for her to face him. Once she was kneeling in front of him, she noticed the nail cutters in his hand.

"What are you doing?" she asked with some hesitation. Not much damage could really be done with nail clippers, especially the travel size ones he held in his hand, but she couldn't count on him not having some devious plan in mind.

"Grooming." He gave her a wicked grin. No hint of malice, just a breathtaking devious smile that knocked the wind from her momentarily. "Give me your hand." He held out his, and wrapped his fingers around hers when she slid it into his palm.

His skin was warm on hers. The callus of his thumb brushed over her knuckle as he singled out her thumb and put the clippers in position.

"I don't even get to keep my nails?" She kept her eyes on the clippers. Never much into the whole girly thing, she didn't pay much attention to her nails. She never painted them or had gotten a manicure, but the idea of having them stripped from her deflated the small balloon of hope that had been building in her.

"If I showed you my back you'd understand. I love it rough, babe, but you took a few more layers off my hide than I find comfortable." He gave her another wink, and kept his mouth turned up in a grin as he finished her thumb and moved on to the next.

He took care, watching every snip as he made it.

"I'm sorry about your back," she whispered as he finished her right hand and gestured for the left.

He gave a small nod, and very briefly connected with her gaze. "I know."

"In all fairness, you were dragging me down to that cage." She looked away, toward the open door leading to the basement.

"You'd just tried to stab me with a screwdriver." His fingers tightened around hers. Deciding it best to keep on his good side, she kept quiet.

"I know this has been a fucked-up month for you. Your brother gets murdered and then I show up." He glanced back up at her. "It's been rough."

"I was there," she said. "When they took him. I'd just walked into his building. Someone slammed the door shut, maybe it was Tommy trying to keep me inside."

Another snip and he collected the nail and placed it on the neat pile he'd started on the table.

"The cops weren't any help." She stiffened as he took her ring finger and positioned her nail between the metal clippers.

"Tommy wasn't one of the good guys, Kara. I know you think he was—"

"No. I don't." She shook her head, keeping her eyes on his fingers. He finished one nail and moved to the next, her fingers remaining stiff as she watched his movements. "I don't know what he did, but I know it wasn't good. But he was my brother. When Mom died, the state tried to take me, wanted to put me in the system. Tommy wouldn't let them, took total custody of me. He didn't have to do that."

Devin paused in his actions and looked up at her. "I get that. No matter how old, an older brother should do whatever it takes to protect his younger sister or brother." Pain underscored his statement. A slight hint, but there nonetheless. Had that been what happened with him and his brother?

He maneuvered the clippers to another nail, and her hand jerked, causing the clippers to slip, snipping too far down. She yelped and yanked her hand away, shaking it in the air.

"Shit." He grabbed her hand and inspected the nail. "You have to hold still, peaches." He took her finger into his mouth, sucking on the tender skin around her nail. As his tongue swirled around the tip of her finger, his eyes watched hers. She couldn't look away. She just stared at him. The tenderness of his touch took her mind away from the pain, smoldering the irritation. Only a few hours ago he'd been hell bent on harming her with that strap. Hadn't he?

He pulled her finger out and examined it again. He kissed the tip of her finger and dropped her hand. "All done." Scooping the nails into his palm, he got up and went to the trash can.

She watched him put the clippers away in a drawer, wash

his hands, and come back to her. When he turned back toward the table, his expression changed. The softness from a moment ago was gone.

"I went to the post office box," he announced as he retook his seat. She looked up at him then. His hands were laced together and dangling between his legs. His elbows rested on his knees. Leaning over to talk with her, his eyebrows raised up naturally, creating several wrinkles on his forehead.

"How did you get a key?" she whispered, already pretty sure she knew the answer.

"Your purse. I grabbed it when we left your apartment. I also have the bag with some of your clothes. You can start earning them by being honest, and working with me." His eyes didn't convey any humor; he wasn't making fun or teasing her. This was his way. Once you lost privileges you earned them back. One by one, she'd have to make her way back to being fully clothed and sleeping in a warm bed. "Do you know what was waiting for you there?"

"No." She shook her head. "Tommy only said that if something happened to him, he went missing, or got arrested, I was to go there and get what he had there for me."

Devin searched her face silently for a minute then gave a small nod. "There were three boxes of envelopes. He'd been paying some guy at the post office to keep everything to the side for him once the post office box filled up. I brought it all back here." He jerked a thumb at the Xerox box on the table.

She craned her neck, trying to see what was inside, but it was too high up for her to see from the position on the floor.

"What did Tommy tell you about his job, about what he did for the Cardone family?"

Cardone? Wasn't that the big boss guy she'd read about in the papers back home from time to time? Was that who Tommy worked for? The Cardone family? "Nothing. We didn't talk about what he did. I knew it was bad, wasn't legal, and I wanted nothing to do with it."

"You never saw anyone come to the apartment, no one came by when you home?"

"I haven't lived with Tommy for four years. I moved out when I turned eighteen. He said it was better, safer for me, because he was starting to get promoted." The words were sour. Tommy liked to talk about what he did like it was a real job, always trying to make her accept it and take the money he supplied.

"So you never met Michael Cardone?"

"No, I don't think so. I stayed away from all of that. Once I moved out, we would get together for dinner now and then, but only at his place if I had to work the late shift. He'd meet me at his place with a pizza or something. Otherwise we just met at a restaurant."

"He wanted to be sure no one knew where you lived?"

"How hard would that really have been?" She gave him a look of annoyance. "Anyone with an internet connection can look up an address." She gave him a pointed look. "I think Tommy just didn't want to bring whatever he was doing to my place. I don't know. I never asked."

"I'm not saying these people are smart, but it seems like your brother was trying to keep you safe. No one ever bothered you, right? So, it must have worked."

"These people? Aren't they your people?" She inched her legs wider to relieve some of the pressure on her knees, dropping her ass between her legs and not caring that the new position left her pussy exposed to him. His eyes weren't on her like some starved beast, not at the moment anyway.

"I don't have people." The way he said it, the harshness of his tone, the chill in his expression as he said it gave her pause. Who the hell was Devin? Not some hired killer, surely. He would have already dispensed with the killing, she supposed, or at least not be showing her any sort of kindness. What would be the need? He could simply rape her if he wanted, then kill her. All this lesson teaching, rule setting, these weren't the actions of some cold-blooded murderer.

"Fine. What is it they want from me now? They've never bothered with me before, Tommy never brought me around them. He had a few friends that showed up at his apartment now and then, but I never really knew them. We didn't socialize. If they showed up, I left. Stupid really. I thought if I cut that part of him away from me, he'd stop, or at least try to get out. You know, so he'd see me more often. But no, he just kept me separate from whatever he was doing and kept working with those people and they killed him. I never even knew their names, a few showed up at his funeral, but none of them talked to me, so why now?"

Devin sat back in his chair, the wood crackling with movement. He grabbed the box and slid it toward him. Out of it he grabbed a few small recorder tapes and a bundle of cash. Hundreds, if she saw correctly. "Your brother was taping conversations, recklessly recording them." Devin waved a tape in the air. "The money? There's at least half a million here, maybe more, I stopped counting."

Half a million? Five hundred thousand dollars? Her mind reeled at that number. She'd never seen that kind of money before, and that was just what he had stashed at the post office box?

"There's also a letter. For you, obviously." He dropped the tape and money back in the box.

"Let me see it," she demanded, thrusting her hand out.

That smirk was back, the one that warned her to back off. "Not so fast, peaches." At least she was back to peaches; she'd take that as a small win. Very small. "First, I'm going to go through all these tapes, see what's there and what isn't. If you're good, very good while I'm doing all of that, I'll get the letter for you."

"You read it?"

"Not yet," he shrugged, as though he couldn't care less what was in it.

"But you will," she snapped.

"Of course I will." The smirk widened, his white teeth showed through. That irritated her. He was so clean and smelled so good, his teeth had been brushed. She, on the other hand, was a complete mess. The hose earlier had left mud splatter all over her legs, her hair could double as a bird's nest, and a disgusting film was starting to grow over her teeth. "Don't look so disappointed. You'll see it, as long as you behave."

An idea came to her. "Look. I don't care about any of this shit. Just take it all and let me go. Whatever they are paying you, five hundred grand has to be more, right? I mean how much is one useless girl really worth to them? Take the money, tell them you did whatever they told you to do, and I'll go away. I won't go back to Chicago, I'll go somewhere else, start over." His face darkened with each word she said but she continued with the plan. "Take it all, Devin. I don't care."

"You'll just disappear?"

"Yes," she nodded, scooting closer to him and placing a hand on his knee. "I'll just go away."

"You'll give me all of this cash and just go somewhere?" His eyes narrowed. "You have no relatives, nothing in your bank accounts, and two changes of clothes." He put his hand over hers when she started to pull back. What did any of that have to do with anything?

"So what? I'll take care of myself." Words she'd spoken so many times to Tommy when he got angry at her for not taking what he offered.

"Take care of yourself." He looked away for a moment; the dark storm brewing in his gaze when he looked back sucked the breath out of her lungs. "Didn't we just talk about this? About how you can't always do that? These aren't some little gang bangers on the street corner. These are bad men, peaches. Real bad. If they got one little doubt that you were out there, walking around knowing things that could put them behind bars, they'll send someone after you. Someone worse than me."

"I'm not your responsibility." She cast her gaze at the floor, unable to meet his eyes. She wasn't anyone's responsibility. He wasn't wrong, she had no one. There was no distant relative to chase after, no money hidden anywhere to save her.

His hand wrapped around the back of her neck, pulling her closer to him. "You are my responsibility, peaches. What did I tell you downstairs? Until I say otherwise, who do you belong to?"

Her mouth dried, and her heart accelerated in her chest. She remembered what he said, remembered how it made her want to believe him. Another self-betrayal. "You. You said I belong to you." Her eyes were locked with his, even if she wanted to look away at that moment, she didn't think she could—his stare was so powerful.

"That's right. Now, you'll be my good girl while I work. No more backtalk, no more fits, no more trying to run away. You did good here, answering my questions." His breath kissed her cheeks, and she found herself craving his lips instead. "I'll let you take a shower. A nice hot shower."

"What are you going to do with me? I don't know anything about what's on those tapes, or what Tommy did for the Cardone family. I'm not a danger to anyone—except apparently myself."

"I'm going to do what I was paid to do, peaches. You'll keep being honest, you'll keep obeying me, and I'll keep you safe from those bad people I told you about."

"When can I go home?"

"Don't think about that right now. Just think about the shower." His fingers gripped her neck harder and brought her closer to him, his lips covering hers. His tongue licked at her lower lip, just enough to gain entry, then swept into her mouth and claimed her. She couldn't stop the shiver of electricity that ran through her body, or the moan that escaped into his mouth. No more could she control her hands from reaching for his shoulders, fisting his shirt than she could make water turn into wine.

When he pulled back, staring down at her with a new smile, a cocky grin, she licked her lips, still tasting him on her skin. "You may take the collar off for your shower, but when you get out, you'll bring it back to me and ask me to put it back on. I won't leash you this time, unless you show me that I need to, and if I need to I'll punish you first."

"You like punishing me, I think."

"There are levels of punishment I enjoy, so do you, but the whipping I gave you earlier—I didn't like that. I don't like those, but they are necessary if my pet gets too far out of line." The backs of his fingers trailed down her cheek. "There are towels and soaps in the bathroom. You may use a towel to dry, but you won't wear it out here. When you are around me, until you've earned your clothes back, you'll be naked. So I can see you, touch you, and enjoy you whenever I want."

"Because I'm your pet." She dropped her gaze, feeling her cheeks heat the instant she said the words, but also feeling the wetness between her legs increase.

"That's right." He kissed her cheek. "Because you're my pet."

CHAPTER TEN

The tapes in the box went back two months. The money, however, had been mailed over the span of four years. Since Kara moved out, Devin supposed. She wouldn't take the drug money he tried to hand her, so he stashed it for her in case something went wrong. And when working for Michael Cardone, something was always bound to go wrong.

Michael kept tabs on all his men, always suspecting someone was out to get him. Even his brother wasn't immune to his big brother's paranoia. It only took one guy in Michael's crew to turn on another for Michael to take action. Looking for evidence before giving the order to get rid of a rat wasn't his style. Making the tapes was a dumbass move, but at least Tommy had the sense not to keep them in his apartment.

It would take days to listen to all the tapes, but he needed to be sure they were clean. That he was clean. Had Michael suspected him of anything, other than the usual paranoid concerns he had regarding everyone? Because when he went into retirement, he didn't want to be looking over his shoulder the rest of his life.

When everything went down, the family would disband, those not related would scatter to the dark recesses of the city until they found more work. This would leave Devin free to disappear as well. Tommy's confession that the tapes existed was enough to put Devin on edge about where he stood with Michael.

The door to the bathroom opened just as Devin slid the first tape into the player. He listened as soft steps came his way in the kitchen. He'd need to start unpacking the boxes in the living room and order the rest of the furniture. The kitchen chairs weren't all that comfortable. Not that she sat on the furniture; she hadn't earned that yet.

Kara was finally starting to listen, to see how it worked between them. He gave the directions, and she obeyed them. He wasn't completely convinced, but for the time being she was being cooperative.

When she stepped into the kitchen he told himself to calm the fuck down. The woman who had been pretty that morning was fucking amazing after the shower. She'd made use of the hair dryer and brush. Most of the curls had been brushed out, leaving a thick wave to her dark, silky locks. Her face was now clean from dirt, sweat, and dried tears, leaving only her fresh, glowing pale skin. Whatever tan she may have sported in the summer months had already faded away.

Her eyes met his for a second before flittering away, somewhere behind him as she walked toward him, holding the collar in one hand. Her cheeks reddened as she held it out to him. He didn't take it from her. No. It wouldn't be that easy, it couldn't be, there had been instructions, and she needed to follow them.

"Oh." The blush deepened when she realized her error. "Will you please put this back on?" She held it up for him again. He still didn't take it, just stood with his hands at his sides, watching her figure out what she did wrong and correct her action again. She sighed and looked him full on. No tears hiding in her eyes this time, no shame. A little annoyance showed there, but he couldn't fault her for that. "Will you please put my collar back on, Sir?"

His lips stretched out into a wide grin, and he took the collar from her. "Of course. Please turn around and lift up your hair."

As she pulled her hair into a ponytail, exposing the soft, pale flesh of her neck, he swallowed back his urge to kiss the tender spot where her shoulder met her throat. One little nibble there, and he would have her complete attention, but he had work to do. He needed to keep his cock down for a little while. He forced himself to focus on pulling the leather strap through the buckle and pinning the small metal bar in place. Sliding two fingers between the collar and her skin, he assured himself that it wasn't too snug, and he made his cock even angrier for not allowing him to indulge in her again.

"There." He patted her shoulder then took a step back to look at her ass. "Now back to your cage while I work." He gave her ass a gentle pat, more to enjoy the slight bounce of her plump flesh than to get her moving, but she didn't need to know that.

"What?" She spun around. "No. I don't want to go back down there. I was good. I ate, I haven't yelled at you or tried to escape. I did everything you said."

"And that's why I allowed you to take a warm shower instead of hosing you off again, peaches." He couldn't let her get the idea she was going to be getting every privilege back just with an hour's obedience. No, it took more than that.

"But I brought the damn collar back to you!" She tugged on the leather strap as though it were strangling her.

"Yes, you did. And for that, I won't leash you. But you are still staying in your cage while I work."

Her eyes lost their softness as she stepped back away from him. Her cheeks flushed with anger, and her hands balled at her sides. "Take me upstairs then. You can cuff me back to the bed." She jerked her thumb at the hallway. "Why the hell not?" she yelled when he shook his head in response.

"First of all, you don't talk to me that way. Second of all, I said you were going back to your cage because that's where you go when you're not behaving. You tried to hurt me, pet. You don't get to sleep in my bed again until we've gotten everything straightened out, when you've learned how to behave."

"I did what you said. I obeyed! What else do you want?" She looked ready to lunge for him, and he braced himself. He hoped she gained control of herself before she did something so stupid. As much as he loved the sway of her ass as he spanked her, she couldn't take another punishment today.

"The idea is to obey even when you don't want to, pet." He walked over to the kitchen pantry and grabbed the damn leash again. She put her hands up, trying to block him, but he was stronger, and managed to get the latch on it. "Let's go." He yanked the lead and practically dragged her to the basement door. When she grabbed onto the door frame and wouldn't let go, he growled. Without even so much as a word to her, he pried her fingers from the frame and hauled her over his shoulder. She gave a little yelp when she landed, but he didn't pay it any mind. They had made progress, but his stubborn little captive wouldn't give over. She wanted to, he'd seen it in her eyes when he encouraged her, when he petted her, but she wasn't letting herself go.

Once inside the cage he gently put her on the floor. "I'll chain you to the damn bars if you give me any trouble. You got me, pet?" He unlatched the leash from the collar and stood up, ready to fight her back to the floor if she jumped at him.

She didn't move. "I hate you." Her arms wrapped around her knees, tucking them tightly to her chest, and her hair fell in front of her face, blocking his view of her expression.

"You want to hate me. But you can't bring yourself to. You hate what I bring out in you, you hate facing your inner desires, but you don't hate me. Any more than I could hate you."

She didn't look up at him, but her arms went tighter around her legs. He'd touched the nerve and exploited her truth.

• • • • • • •

Kara leaned back against the bars of her cage, trying to remember the lyrics to a pop song she had memorized as a teen. New Kids on the Block were the in thing back then, and she had loved all five of the young pop stars. Every lyric of every song had been embedded in her brain, but as she sat in her cell, captive and alone, she couldn't remember all of them.

What else was she going to do? It had been a full day since Devin locked her back in that jail. Twenty-four hours since she'd eaten her lunch like a good pet from a dog bowl, and had done so since as well. Because even though she stopped talking to him, stopped trying to get to of the cage, he'd not given an inch. How the hell was she supposed to earn privileges if he didn't tell her how? And worse, the part that made her hate him the most, why was she so damn eager to get in his good graces again?

Before she'd yelled at him in the kitchen, she'd enjoyed the moments of peace between them. He didn't give off such an asshole vibe. She tried not to remember his hands on her, petting her, stroking her while she ate because it would start to tear into the wall she wanted to create. He continued to do that, whenever he fed her. He hadn't taken her back upstairs, but he'd brought her food and water down to her. He would sit in a chair while she knelt beside him and ate. He'd stroke her hair and her back; a few times he'd even ventured lower. Telling her to part her legs a little for him.

"That's my good girl," he'd said and slipped a finger into her pussy while she ate. She moaned right into the damn noodles while he finger fucked her the whole way through her meal. And just as she finished eating, he pulled his finger out and thrust it into her mouth, calling it dessert. She'd been so damn aroused, she'd lapped up all the juices, hoping that he would finish what he started. But he didn't. He just snapped his fingers and pointed back to the damn cage. At least he didn't make her crawl.

The door opened upstairs, and she heard the familiar sound of him jogging down the stairs. When he hopped off the last step she looked him over. He wasn't wearing anything aside from a black pair of cargo pants. She hadn't seen so much of him until that moment. His chest and abdomen were sculpted like something she'd seen in men's fitness magazines. His arms were just as muscular, with tattoos running down both of them. His feet were bare.

"Pet." He stalked over to her cage, around to where she sat and crouched down to meet her gaze. She wanted to look away. She should have avoided his eyes, but they were so… hungry. "What have you been doing down here all day?" he asked, resting his elbows on his knees and folding his hands.

"Thinking of ways to kill you." She regretted the remark as soon as she said it. It was a joke. But seeing the small injury on his arm from where she tried to do just that, she realized how bad of one it was.

"Ah, well, if I were you, I'd be thinking about ways to start earning privileges back. I mean I'm sure it's nice to pee in a toilet, and you've gotten the shower back, but I bet a bed would be sweet right about now. A blanket maybe?"

"What do you want?" she sighed. "I haven't been any trouble."

"No, you haven't. You've kept quiet, you've not talked back, you've been very docile," he admitted. "I've finished going through the tapes. But it's not good. Not for either of us. I need you to get that, you have to understand that we are both in danger."

"Why you?"

"Doesn't matter. What does matter is I want to play.

Does my pet want to play, too?" He reached his arm through the cage and stroked her hair. The warm touch of his fingers should have pissed her off, but once more she found herself leaning into his touch.

"I want out of this cage." She kept her voice soft; better to play his game than fight him.

"Good." He stood up and unbuttoned the cargo pants. She watched as he lowered his zipper and pulled out his cock. His long, thick, hard cock. He stroked himself while staring down at her. Her tongue ran over her lips as she watched him, her heart starting to race and the rest of her body urging her forward. She knew what he wanted, what she needed to do if she was to get out of the cage.

If only the act repulsed her as much as it should have. If he wouldn't look at her with such desire, maybe she could refuse.

Instead, she found herself moving to the bars, up onto her knees, bringing her face to the same height as his cock. While he'd been working on whatever he'd been working on, she'd been alone. So alone, wishing for him to show up, show his face. Even a punishment would have been better than the isolation.

But that was his point, she figured. Behave or she'd be left in her cage with nothing but her thoughts. During the time she'd been alone, she'd thought of him, of the way his fingers made her feel, the way his belt made her ass burn, made her pussy weep for him. It was a mess; she was a mess. Once out of the hell she sat in, she'd need a team of therapists to fix her. What sort of person craved her captor in the way she was beginning to crave him? Just the sound of his voice brightened her mood, and to see him walk into the room and actually talk with her could send her skyrocketing. It was classic; she was falling for him because he was her kidnapper and he'd completely isolated her from everything in the outside world.

He said they were in danger. Not just her, but him as well. Did that make him less of an asshole? He had what he wanted, the tapes, she wasn't going to even try to take the money in that box, it was his. All he had to do was let her go; instead, he'd tossed her back in the cage.

"Do you want something, pet?" His rough voice rolled over her body as well as any fingertip or lips. His lips. He hadn't kissed her since they were in the kitchen; in fact, other than the finger fucking during her breakfast he hadn't touched her at all.

She licked her lips again, telling herself that sucking his cock meant she'd be able to get out of the cage. It was just a means to an end, nothing else. She told herself that, but even she knew she was a bullshitter.

"I—" Her eyes darted up to his, not wanting to ask, or say what she wanted, and hoping like hell he wouldn't make her.

"Oh, I think you can do better than that. Tell me. Ask me to suck my cock. It's what you want, isn't it? To suck me hard, lick me, and have your face fucked with it?" Back was the crude jackass from the truck. Maybe what he'd heard on those tapes was bad. Maybe he'd come down for stress relief, something to soothe him. And fuck her, she wanted to give him that. Because if they were in trouble, if he was telling her the truth, she couldn't think of anyone else who would be helping her. His brother? Maybe, depended on how dirty of a cop he was, or how good of a brother.

The man stood before her, looking for a way to relieve his worry. The man who promised to protect her from the bad guys, even if that meant locking her away for her own good.

She inched toward him, reaching through the bars until her hands rested on his thighs. The firmness of his muscles there told her how hard he worked to maintain his body. No one got quads like that from doing a handful of squats; no, he was disciplined in his schedule.

"Let me." She licked her lips again, keeping her eyes mingling with his. The edges of his stare softened. He'd been looking for a fight, or at least expecting one. She'd had enough fighting. Her soul was tired, her body ached, she wanted to find the middle ground with him. The small strip of peace they could reside in together to get through whatever fucked-up shit her brother had put her in.

He shuffled closer to the bars, his cock nearly through the space where her mouth was positioned. "Open your mouth, stick out your tongue," he ordered. One final lick of her lips, and she spread them, jutting her tongue out past her teeth. "Don't close your mouth, not even your lips. This mouth is mine, understand?"

Even if her mind didn't, her pussy got the idea just fine. She could feel the wetness already slipping between her lower lips, knowing if she touched her clit she'd find it engorged with her arousal, and most likely ready to come.

The soft round head of his cock touched her outreached tongue, sliding over it and going deeper into her mouth. Her throat started to clench, but she worked the muscles and swallowed, opening for him and keeping the gag at bay. Fuck, he was a lot bigger than she remembered. Just as she felt the back of her throat clenching again, he pulled back. Before she could take a deep breath, he thrust forward, hitting the back of her throat once more and eliciting a gag.

"Fuck." She pulled her head back and coughed, then quickly got back into position.

"Good girl, but no cursing. I don't like it, and I'll wash your mouth out with soap next time you do it." His threat, or rather his promise, didn't fall on deaf ears. She'd have to watch her foul mouth, but it would be hard. A bad habit she only seemed able to curb while at work, and even then she let her guard down when patients weren't in earshot. "Open your mouth wider, pet. I want you to take my whole cock in. Stick out your fucking tongue, or I'll hold it out for you."

Whatever means he would use to do that, she wanted no part of. She readjusted her knees on the floor, then opened again, wider and stuck her tongue out further. Immediately his cock shoved into her mouth, hitting the back of her throat. But when she tried to pull away again, his hands flew through the bars and clenched her hair, holding her to him. She coughed and sputtered, but finally managed to relax her throat enough to let him settle into her without choking. He moved further, and further still until her nose touched the nest of pubic hair at the base of his cock.

"Ah, fuck!" He pulled back, letting her take a deep breath then plunged in again, and again, he fucked her throat as aptly as he would her pussy. She gripped his thighs, holding on as her breath was stolen then replaced. Her eyes began to water as his cock hit the back of her throat again. The droplets trickled out the corner of her eyes, trailing down her cheeks, but she made no move to wipe them. Her focus remained on his cock; the feel, the taste, the fullness of it as he used her throat to his benefit—and to hers. "Good girl." He moved one hand from her hair and cupped her chin, held her lower jaw down, and fucked her faster.

She could feel his balls tighten as they slapped her chin, his thighs trembled as he continued to plow into her mouth. "Close your lips, suck hard." He released her chin, and she wrapped her lips tightly around his shaft, sucking harder than she'd ever done with a man before. Her experience was limited, but Devin didn't seem the gentle blowjob type. When he said suck hard, he meant it.

He yanked his cock out and her lips made a popping sound. "Again." He shoved his cock back through her lips before she could even part them for him. Another popping sound. He did this several times, before grasping her hair again, holding her down on him. She slapped his thighs, signaling her need for air, and he pulled her off, giving her what she needed at that moment. She held her head steady as he took what he wanted from her. After half a dozen more strokes, he held steady in her mouth. Hot, salty come burst from his cock, splashing her tongue and the walls of her mouth. "Drink it. All of it," he managed to say through his clenched teeth. She swallowed, the movement of her throat eliciting more come from his dick.

Once he was completely spent, he released her hair. Her

scalp burned from his fingers, but she didn't rub away the sting, or comment on it. He pulled free of her mouth, letting his dick dangle in front of her lips, the smell of his come still fresh on his flesh. "Clean it up, pet."

She licked him. God help her, she licked his cock as though it were a Popsicle in the middle of July in the city. Once every drop of his come had been retrieved by her whore's tongue, she wiped her mouth with the back of her hand.

"That's a good pet." He patted her head and tucked his cock back into his pants. He didn't say anything else, he just moved to the door of her cage and unlocked it. "There's a robe upstairs on the kitchen table. You may put it on while we eat." He left the door open and walked out of the room, up the stairs.

He was letting her upstairs. With a robe, and no leash? Her lips curled into a smile. She was going to be warm again. For at least a few minutes.

CHAPTER ELEVEN

The first blowjob Devin ever had consisted of three strokes of the girl's hand and about two strokes with her mouth before he combusted all over the place, mostly on her face and her shirt. He'd had several years of practice since then, and learned to control himself better. Up until he slid his cock into that gorgeous mouth of Kara's. Fuck, she had a body he couldn't stop staring at, a mind he wanted to wrap himself in, and a mouth he wanted to die inside of.

Things were going to get out of hand if he couldn't pull himself together. It was one thing to use the girl to relieve some stress, she had even seemed to understand what was going on. But it was another to start thinking about all the things he loved… no, liked about her.

Leaving her in the basement for the past day had been more torture on him than her, of that he had no doubt. He missed her smart-ass remarks. Hell, he missed just having her sit by him. But it had been necessary. He needed to listen to all the tapes, to see what bullshit web her brother spun.

Too many things he'd said on the tapes were lies, ways of him trying to cover his own fucking tracks by throwing other people under the bus. Unfortunately for Devin, he was one of the less fortunate. Twice he'd implicated him in a murder, and once he talked about the plan for his taking over the family. If the tapes got into the hands of the cops, Devin could be pegged for the murders. If they made their way to Michael, he'd be pegged for a traitor. Tommy hadn't been completely dumb. Either way this all went down it wasn't going to be smooth sailing.

But what had him pissed the most was the way he tossed his own fucking sister under with him. He'd mentioned her here and there, nothing big, nothing to really warrant anyone being worried about her. But he dropped little clues that if anything ever happened to him, his little sister had his back. The fucking idiot. No wonder Michael wanted her out of the picture for good. Just turning over the tapes wouldn't be enough for him, he'd already said it, but after listening to the evidence, Devin knew damn sure she couldn't go back home. Not with Michael in charge of the family.

There was good reason for Michael to be paranoid about someone always trying to heist him out of his seat as the head. Under his leadership the family made money, yes, but only Michael saw the vast wealth of it. Everyone else took in enough to be more than comfortable. But why put up with fifty percent when you really were entitled to seventy-five percent?

If the tapes were ever released for the rest of the family to hear, Michael would have more to worry about than some DA having more evidence to put him away. He'd be a fucking target for his own family. That could work to Devin's advantage, but he had to be careful. It wasn't just his life he was trying to save.

"Devin?" The soft voice of hers traveled from the kitchen to where he was unpacking boxes in the front room. He paused, keeping silent. A test. Would she run for the front door or the back? "Devin?" Closer she stepped in his direction. "Where are you?"

Her shadow appeared along the stairwell before she came into view. The black robe he'd left out for her covered her body, except for her calves. And until he saw her standing in his robe, he never would have believed a set of calves could set his libido into full drive.

From where Devin stood, behind a tower of boxes, she didn't see him clearly. Her eyes darted to the door, and she stood there, wringing her hands. She might make it to the truck, but he had the keys. Never would she outrun him in bare feet. And there was still the matter of her nudity beneath the robe. Decisions. Decisions.

Her face twisted into an expression of pained thought. She was torn. Run or stay. He crouched down, being sure to stay out of her line of sight. She needed to make this call.

"Fuck." She cursed and stomped her right foot, the sound nearly nonexistent against the hardwood flooring. "Devin?" she called louder, turning toward the steps.

"Here!" He stepped out of his hiding space holding a few books in his hands. "I'm here, what's up?" *What's up? She's your fucking captive, dumbass, and she's looking for you. How much more twisted do you need the situation to get before you finally clue her into the whole mess?*

"You said to meet you—what are you doing?" She stepped into the room, peering at the boxes. They'd been stored in the barn when they had arrived days earlier. He'd just brought them in that morning.

"What's it look like? Unpacking." He turned to put the books on the built-in bookcase and wiped his hands on his cargo pants.

"For your retirement?" Her lips twisted into a soft smile as she lifted a small statue portraying a woman on her knees, her hands cupped and over her head. It was one piece of a set. The woman's dominant completed the pair and was probably in the same box.

"Yes." He closed the gap between them with two long strides and snatched the artwork from her hands. A friend had created them for him specifically; he didn't want them broken.

"So this is like your house then?" She began to walk between the boxes, peeking into the opened ones and checking the writing on the sealed.

"Something like that."

"And the cabins?" she asked, looking out of the front bay window. They weren't finished. The frames were up, but the insides hadn't been completed. Though the row of cabins that ran along the property line weren't visible from the window she was looking out of.

"How'd you know about those?"

"I heard your brother. You two should talk softer if you don't want your voices to travel."

He carried the two statues to the bookcase and placed them where he wanted them. "The door was closed."

"Might want to get a thicker door then," she shrugged and continued with her exploration. "So what are the cabins for? You going to start a vacation resort? After you've finished my kidnapping and all that?"

If he hadn't just used her mouth for his own personal fuck vessel, he'd think she was flirting with him. Her eyes certainly twinkled as though she were, but that couldn't be. No, she was his toy, his pet. This, this casual talk, this was her way of being civil so she wouldn't end up locked in her cage again.

Her cage. How quickly he'd come to think of it as that, completely hers. Would he be able to use it again after she was gone? Could he really lock up another woman in her cage and not think of her the entire time they played?

"What else did you hear?" He thought back to the conversation with Trevor, searching for anything that might give away too much.

"Just that really." She turned away from the windows and hugged herself around her stomach. The robe accented the sleek lines of her shoulders, and the belt around her waist exposed her most feminine curves. "I fell asleep." Her confession reddened her cheeks, and she abruptly turned her back on him and started to head out of the room. "I thought we were having lunch."

"I think that robe has given you your boldness back," he

observed out loud. Gone was the timid woman he'd encountered downstairs in her cage.

She turned back to him at the doorway, dropping her gaze. "I'm hungry."

"And you think you've earned it because you sucked my cock like a good girl?" He grinned as he asked the question, thoroughly enjoying the reddened cheeks and how she sucked her lower lip between her teeth. He stepped over a box and walked up to her, lifting her hand to link their fingers together. "Your shame has no place here, peaches. You didn't do anything wrong. Nothing you do with me will be wrong. Besides, if you do, you know I'll strap that perfect ass of yours. So you let me worry about the bad stuff, and you just keep going on as you have the past day." He gave her hand a little squeeze and pulled her along to the kitchen.

What difference did it really make if she was ashamed or not? Once he was finished, once she was free of him, she'd have a lot more to worry about than feeling a little slutty. But he couldn't let her think what she did was anything but good. Because it was anything but bad.

He pointed to the chair to the right of where he usually sat and left her to get the sandwiches he made out of the fridge. When he turned back to her, she was sitting on the edge of the chair, as though she wasn't really sure she was doing the right thing or not.

"Scoot back or you'll tip over." He shot her a little smile and put her sandwich in front of her. He watched as she peeled back the bread to inspect the insides. "Just ham and mustard," he mumbled as he bit into his own lunch.

"Is your brother coming back?" she asked, sniffing the sandwich. He watched her with curiosity when she finally took a small bite. A tiny breadcrumb rested on her bottom lip while she chewed. When she didn't wipe her hand across her mouth, he reached over and ran his thumb over the lip, wiping the crumb away. She pulled back a little at his touch, bringing her own hand to touch her mouth.

"No. He's not." Devin wiped his hand on his pants and

went back to eating.

"It doesn't bother him? You know, that you're a criminal?"

"Lots of things I do bother him." He shot her a look that suggested she drop the topic.

"Like you being a criminal?" He would have been angry, could have easily ripped the robe off of her for her impertinence and brattiness, except she gave him an innocent smile that told him she was being anything but. The woman *was* flirting, although he had a damn good feeling she didn't know it.

He didn't answer, just gave a pointed look at her uneaten sandwich. Once she started eating it, he popped the last bit of his own in his mouth and picked up his plate, taking it to the sink. Leaning against the counter, he folded his arms over his chest and crossed his right ankle over his left, watching her. Just his gaze on her turned her cheeks pink, though she did her best not to look at him. The struggle was there in her eyes. Glancing over at him when he had obviously ended the conversation might give him the impression she was looking for his attention, and she wouldn't want him to get that idea—so he kept looking at her. Letting her know she had his undivided attention.

"When you retire, you'll live here then?" She still didn't look at him. Her soft brown eyes settled on his chest, though the coloring of her cheeks darkened the longer she stared at his muscular build. He wasn't obtuse. Girls admired his physique, and he'd be a lying bastard if he said he didn't appreciate their stares.

"Finish your lunch. I have to get back to work, so you need to go—"

"No." The curls of her hair bounced as she shook her head.

"No?" He couldn't help the laugh in his voice. A little food and a robe and the girl went right back to being defiant and stubborn. Which one of them was learning the lessons here?

"I mean, please no." Ah, so she had learned something. At least she was using some manners with her defiance. "I can help you unpack." Although the offer was given as a way to stay out of her cage, it still held some promise. It would give her something to do, and he could keep an eye on her while he got work done.

"If I let you stay out of your cage, what will you do for me?"

"I-I just said, I can help you unpack." Her eyes fluttered across his chest, then sank lower, following the muscles of his abdomen, until they settled on the bulge in his pants. Even after having just fucked her throat not an hour before, he was ready to go again. Something about her made his blood boil and his cock crave her at the same time. A lesser man would have probably fallen under her little spell by now, but not him.

"I don't really need your help with that," he pointed out. Sure it would go faster, but he didn't need it.

"I—well, I could, like downstairs." Her cheeks were nearly crimson with the suggestion, but it wasn't bold enough. Not by a long shot.

"Now, you can do better than that, I think, peaches." He lifted the side of his mouth and waited as she searched her brain for a better offer.

"Whatever you want?" Ding! It didn't really matter what she offered him, he would do just that anyway. Whatever the fuck he wanted, because she belonged to him.

"Whatever I want." He scratched his chin, mocking deep thought. He already knew what he wanted, little thought was actually needed. "I want your obedience."

"I've been good." She started to twist her fingers together in her lap.

"You've been good because I left you alone. Hard to misbehave in a cage all by yourself." He uncrossed his ankles. "But let's check your theory. Stand up."

• • • • • • •

Kara's stomach twisted again at his command. Maybe she should have run for the door. She might have made it to a road, or a neighbor. But instead, she hadn't risked it. She'd been good and called for him, and what did it get her? Not a whole lot. A ham sandwich.

"Pet." The warning in his voice got her legs moving. She shoved the chair back and got to her feet, holding tight to the robe around her waist. Completely a placebo, her mind knew it, but still she held onto the belt of the robe as though it were a steel shield. "Good. Now untie the robe, and remove it." See? What was the point of letting her wear it if he was just going to take it away from her?

Not wanting to go back to the solitary of the damn cage, she decided to follow his directions. What's the worst that could happen? He could fuck her again, and would that really be so damn bad? As sick as it was to want his cock inside of her, she had to admit she'd had the best sex and the most sex in the past few days with him than she had had in the last several years.

Untying the robe at a snail's pace, she kept her eyes away from him. She didn't need to look to know he was staring at her, and if she saw him, saw those eyes peering at her with sure satisfaction at her obedience, she didn't trust her reaction. The idea to stay out of the cage kept her temper in check, and her mind focused just on the next few moments. Just get through the next minute then think about what comes next. Just the next minute, she could get through sixty seconds; she could do anything for sixty seconds.

"Drop the robe, pet." His damn voice intervened in the middle of her pep talk. Letting the soft material slide down her arms, she exposed her body to him. No different than the first time she'd bared her body, except this time, she wasn't as ashamed, there was no nervousness about what he thought, or what he would do. Only the vulnerability remained as before. In this state of complete undress, he could stare at her most intimate parts, touch any part of her body he wished, grope, kiss, lick, slap. Spank. Her ass had finally stopped throbbing from the whippings she'd taken. Only slight tenderness remained, and she wasn't in the mindset to change that.

When he remained silent, she chanced a quick peek. He hadn't moved, but his eyes were roaming her body. She bit the inside of her cheek to keep from covering herself from him. He wouldn't approve if she did, and it wouldn't matter, he'd just make her move her hands anyway. Keeping her hands down was her choice; not his, but hers. At least she let herself continue with that belief, knowing it wasn't the truth. He had told her before, on the first day he took her that she wouldn't have choices anymore, not real ones. Only the choice to obey. That was her choice. And it seemed he kept true to his word. He'd stripped away every other real choice from her. If she obeyed, she was given her privileges back, and if she chose not to, he took them away. A simple formula really.

"Good. Now bend over the table, keep your ass high in the air for me, pet."

"I-I was good. I didn't do anything." The words were out before she thought better.

He didn't respond, other than to raise one eyebrow and continue staring at her. Obey his command or not, that was her choice in that moment. That's what he was impressing upon her.

Silently she bent over the table, her palms pressed on the cool wood, her breasts flattened by the surface, she lifted her ass up into the air, almost on her tiptoes to make it work. At first there was no sound in the kitchen. She turned her head to face him. He wasn't there.

The temptation to get up grew as the moments ticked by, but he wouldn't have gone far. He could be in the doorway. Or the pantry. He stepped out of the pantry carrying a small bottle of olive oil in one hand. He placed the bottle on the table, right in front of her eyes. The question of what it was for teetered on her tongue, but his hands on her ass stilled her mind.

Wooden legs scraping the kitchen floor signaled him moving the chair behind her. One hand on each of her ass cheeks, he rubbed her skin tenderly. "The welts are all but gone. Good." He patted her rump. "Let's not repeat those punishments."

When he remained silent she figured he expected a reply. "Yes, Sir." The words slipped out of her mouth with more ease than she would have liked.

"Ah, good girl." He patted her ass again, sounding genuinely pleased with her. "Now. Let's see if you can keep being a good girl for me. No matter what, you keep your position. Understood, peaches? You don't move until I say so, and you sure as hell don't come unless you have permission."

Come? So he was going to fuck her. Well, fine. If she had to put up with his little games, at least the ache inside of her would be relieved. "Yes, Sir. I understand. Don't move." She nodded, though he couldn't see her.

Without another word, he pried her ass cheeks apart. Far apart. She started to bolt upright, but the tsking of his tongue stilled her. She pressed herself further into the table, reminding herself nothing he did would kill her, and nothing he did would be worse than that razor strap.

"I'm just looking. Has anyone looked at you here?" The very tip of a finger tapped her puckered hole.

"N-no, Sir." She clenched her eyes closed, and her bottom, hoping to hide what she could from him.

"Relax, pet. That won't work anyway. I'm going to have my finger in there soon enough; your cooperation is only important for your comfort, not my ability." Of course he would have his way, her choices remained the same. Obey or not. *Fuck.*

"Please." The tears were already welling up in her eyes, and he hadn't done anything more than look at her. He was going to stick his finger in her ass, which fully explained the oil, but would he then force his cock in there, too?

A boyfriend once tried to fuck her in the ass, though he was a little less concerned about lube. He had spit on his cock and then tried to ram it in before she could figure out what was going on. One minute he was pounding into her from the back, the next he had pulled out. Full force, he'd jammed his cock into her ass, but it didn't get far. The first sensation of her ass being painfully stretched had her leaping across the bed, landing on a heap on the floor. That relationship didn't last very long after that.

"If no one's looked at you here, then no one's fucked you here?" The finger massaged the clenched ring of muscle, her cheeks still unreasonably spread before his eyes. "I want an answer, pet." Without moving his finger, he pinched her cheek, the tender flesh right above her hole.

"Not really, no."

"Not really? What does that mean?" The massaging continued.

She could have simply answered with no; now she would have to explain what had happened. Being her own worst enemy wasn't working so well for her. "A boyfriend tried once. It didn't work." His fingers deepened their grip on her cheeks, spreading her even further than she thought possible as he started to massage harder against the tight ring.

"How did it not work?" One hand moved away, her cheek dropping back into normal position, only to be pulled back again and a cool liquid ran down the crack of her ass. He'd poured the damn oil on her. His finger began the massaging again, only softer, and more concentrated on one area. "Answer me." The command was given a bit softer than his others, as his finger began to press inward on her, trying to breach the tight pucker.

"He didn't use anything, he just shoved."

"Relax your asshole, peaches. You can't keep me out, and I'd rather you enjoyed this. Because later, when you've been opened for me, I'm going to fuck you here. Whether you enjoy it or not, that's your decision. But I'm thinking enjoying your ass fucking is better than not." What sort of choice was that? Not much of one; again it boiled down to obedience. He was going to do what he wanted, and she only had to decide on how she would accept it.

She tried to relax, but every time she started to feel her muscles give, his finger pushed harder and she clamped up again. A hot sting of a slap met her cheek.

"Push out." His finger popped through the tight rim and the burn of the invasion made her moan. He couldn't have been in very deep, but enough for her to feel her face catch flame from the embarrassment. She was leaned over a fucking table while he had a finger in her ass. Eating from the damn dog bowl did not compare to this new humiliation, and she hadn't even earned this one. "That's my girl." Damn him for using those words. "Now, tell me more, what happened."

"He tried, it didn't work." She ground her teeth together as his finger began to move. He pushed forward, then moved out before pushing forward again.

"No, tell me everything. Why didn't it work?"

"He didn't tell me he what he was going to do; he just shoved at me." A tear slipped out of her clenched eyelids. The more his finger moved, the less burning stretch she felt. It morphed too quickly into a comfortable ache.

"No lube?" His finger stilled.

"No. He just spit on himself then shoved." She didn't want to talk about it. That guy had been a complete selfish prick. She knew it, but had hoped he'd change. But men didn't change. No one did. The whole incident had been her own fault for thinking he would have her best interest in heart.

"You didn't talk about trying it first? He just surprised you like that?" His voice had changed. He sounded irritated, but she hadn't done anything wrong. She wasn't fighting him anymore; her muscles were as relaxed as she was going to get them with his finger stuck in her the way it was.

"Yeah, but it didn't work. I jumped away." More like

flew, right over the bed and onto the floor, bumping her elbow on the nightstand and giving herself a nice bruise for the trouble.

For several moments, silence hung in the air. His finger didn't move anymore, and he hadn't said anything. "Well, he was a fucking moron. He could have really hurt you doing shit like that." Again, he pushed his finger forward, going deeper than before. She moaned, throwing her head back. She wasn't supposed to be enjoying it, but there she was and damn her if she wasn't started to push back toward him to take his finger even further. "How long did you date him?"

"After that, only a few days." She arched her back, hoping he'd touch her clit. She could feel the heaviness in her sensual nub, it needed some attention, too.

"Did he ever hurt you other than that?"

She rested her forehead against the table. He slowly eased a second finger into her ass, making her feel more full and ache for more attention to her clit. She wiggled her ass a little, trying to get him to see her need. "Pet. Did he ever hurt you other than that?"

"No. Not really. He was a jerk, but he never used a strap on my ass if that's what you mean." The regret for her words was immediate. He wouldn't reward her for that, he might not touch her clit at all if she kept talking to him like that.

"I didn't hurt you. I wounded your pride, I made your ass sore, but I didn't harm you. What I'm doing now isn't harming you. It may hurt a little. It may make you feel a little humbled to have my fingers in your ass, stretching you and taking you as I want, but you aren't being injured." To prove his point, he reached beneath her with his free hand and began to pet her cunt, brushing over her clit and sending her endorphins into overdrive.

Again, her back arched, her ass pushed against his fingers, and she ground her pelvis into his hand. Her clit swelled even more beneath his touch.

"Why are you doing this?" Her mind whirled as he

continued to stroke her sensitive pussy and push inward into her ass. He didn't answer her, he just kept pushing and pushing and rubbing until both of his fingers were inside of her ass, filling her up. Scissoring his fingers, he stretched her even more and the initial burn began again, but this time it didn't feel painful. This time it sent more sensations to her clit and made the rubbing he was doing there more intense.

"Doing what? Playing with your asshole? Touching your pussy? Or something deeper? Why am I keeping you here, protecting you?" His fingers probed deeper, harder.

Figuring he wanted an answer, she tried to concentrate hard enough to put words together. "Yes."

He laughed, a soft chuckle that expressed exactly how pleased he was with her compromising position.

"I'm finger fucking your asshole and pussy because I want to—because you love it. Your body hums when I stroke it, did you realize that? Your pupils dilate, your skin softens beneath me, like it was made for my touch." He slowed his thrusts. "I'm protecting you because you need it. Because it's my job." He cursed under his breath. "Because I would be very unhappy if something bad happened to you."

Not exactly Shakespeare, but the sentiment filled her heart nonetheless. Nothing would come of it—his feelings, or her own. Nothing could.

His fingers moved quicker, her clit was given more attention. Distractions were best given in sensual form, she decided.

"Devin. Sir." She pushed her pelvis harder into his hand, needing more friction, wanting more heat from him.

The buildup of her orgasm began to weigh down on her. He said she couldn't come unless he gave her permission. Would he give it freely or would she have to ask? She wasn't sure she'd be able to ask, not with his fingers causing too many feelings. She bit her lower lip and looked over her shoulder at him. His eyes were on her; he wasn't even looking at what his fingers were doing. Assessment, that's what he was doing. Taking assessment of her reactions. And as usual when he touched her, she'd turned into a raving whore.

Another pass of his finger over her clit and she bucked back at him, needing more and hating it.

"Do you want something, pet? Do you want to come? Like this? Bent over my table, your pussy being played with while my fingers are in your ass? Can you feel how full you are? I have two whole fingers in there, fucking your ass. Imagine what my cock will feel like." The man knew what his words were going to do, he knew that in that tone with those words he could make her putty in his hands. Why was she so easy? After years of putting up walls, of making sure she was safe, she could crumble so easily in this man's hands because of a few words?

"Please." She pushed harder against him, needing his fingers to be rougher. He obliged and thrust his fingers harder into her, twisting them and fucking her again. "Please." It was as much as she would say; she wouldn't beg him. Not the way he wanted.

"Please what? Full question or I'll stop."

Stop? No, he couldn't leave her like that. "Please, may I… I need to…" She tried to catch her breath, to focus her thoughts but he timed the fingers in her ass with his fingers on her clit so that she never received a second of peace. Just pleasure and burning joy with each passing moment. "Can I come?" she finally spit out, finding the edge of the table with her hands and gripping hard to keep herself from throwing her body at him and really begging for him to fuck her in the ass. Because that's what she wanted. She wanted him to pull down his pants, pull out that thick cock of his, and fuck her hard in her ass. To take her as his own, because she was his pet, she was his to do with as he wanted. "Please, Sir, may I come?" Between her quickened breath, her mind getting foggier as the moments passed, she wasn't even sure he understood her.

"You want to come? Will you be my good girl from now

on?"

"Yes!" She gripped the table harder, pushed her ass further out. "I'll be your good girl." She nodded. "Please, Sir. Please." She was begging, dammit. But her body didn't care, her body wanted to obey him, to follow him and get the rewards of his pleasure. Her mind wanted it, too; the very carnal part of her mind wanted to hear him call her a good girl, to pet her hair and sit with her.

"Come for me then. That's it, fuck my fingers." He stopped moving his fingers in her ass, making her do all of the work. She moved her hands from the edge of the table, to flatten them on the wood surface, lifting herself off the table. Pushing hard back at him, she began to do just as he asked; she fucked his fingers, harder and harder, faster until the pressure was too great to hold anymore. As though he knew exactly what her body wanted, he rubbed her clit harder, flicking it lightly then grinding his fingers into her until she couldn't contain a sense of reality.

She screamed out her orgasm. Yelling out into the room, with each forceful wave of pleasure that rocketed through her body. Not letting up, she fucked his fingers even harder, riding out the entirety of the explosion. It went on for long moments that felt more like minutes, maybe even longer. She cursed, she cried, she wasn't sure what the hell she was saying, but when it finally passed and she felt her body start floating back down to the real world, she collapsed onto the table in a heap of a mess. A thin sheen of sweat covered her face, and a few strands of hair were matted to her forehead.

As she tried to catch her breath, gulping in air as she went, he eased his fingers from her backside and reached beside her where a towel she hadn't noticed before sat. The chair scraped again and the towel reappeared on the table. "Come here, pet." His soft command was coupled by his hands on her waist pulling her to sit in his lap.

He turned her so that he could cradle her, and pushed her head to rest against his chest. On instinct, she wrapped her arms around his neck and burrowed beneath his chin.

Warm arms wrapped around her, adjusting her on his lap until they were both comfortable. She could feel the tears coming, but held no power to stop them. They flowed, and her shoulders shook, and she cried. Really cried. Sat on his lap—her abductor, her owner—and sobbed into his bare chest.

"Shhhh, it's okay. I know it's been a rough week for you, but it's going to be okay." He brushed her hair off her face.

What was there to say to that? She cried until she was done. When her body was left with nothing but an ache that covered her from head to toe, and the entire time he just held her. He didn't get irritated that her nose was running, or that his chest was all wet with her tears. He didn't reprimand her for crying like a baby while he held her as one. He just held her until she was depleted. And then, he picked her up and carried her back downstairs.

Not to the cage. She'd tensed at the sight of it, but he'd just patted her bottom and took her over to the bed, laying her down on the soft mattress. He pulled out a washcloth from the small nightstand beside it and cleaned up her face. No stern words or mockery, just a gentle cleaning. She tried to watch his expression for disgust or repulsion, but all she saw was concern and nurturing.

Once her face was cleaned off, he slid into the bed beside her, pulling her against him. She laid her cheek against his chest, listening to the sound of his heart beating and wondering what to do next. Sniffling, she rubbed her eyes with her hand and snuggled closer to him. "I promise you'll come out of this okay."

"You won't spank me anymore?" She barely had the energy to whisper her question.

His chest rumbled with a chuckle. "If you earn a spanking, you'll get a spanking."

"Why?"

With soft fingers, he pulled her hair up and began twirling it. "Because it's how you're built. You may not want to be taken care of, you think the world rests comfortably on your shoulders, but it doesn't have to be that way. You think it makes you weak to accept help. You want to serve, to help others, but you won't take what they offer in return."

"You aren't making any sense." She tried not to, but the yawn escaped nonetheless. Her eyelids grew heavier as they talked.

"You've wanted to be under a man's control for a very long time, but have only been around men who couldn't even control themselves, much less you. Your brother, your boyfriends—they all needed you because they weren't men enough to take care of themselves. You've been seeing to your own needs for so damn long, you've almost forgotten how to let someone else do it. Besides, even if your mind won't let you admit it yet, you love it. You hate that you do, but you do. It's time to put your mind quiet and listen to your body, to your heart."

"You kidnapped me." She reminded him with closed eyes, her body softened against his, knowing that for the moment she was safe.

"It seemed that way, I know. I need you to start trusting me, really listening to me because things are going to get messy really quick now. If you can do that then we will both get out of this whole fucking mess in one piece."

"You don't make sense again." She snuggled further into his embrace.

Warm lips pressed against her forehead. "Sleep, peaches. You need rest, then we'll go over what's coming next."

Another yawn captured her attention and she nodded, not really registering what he was talking about. "You're going to fuck my ass," she whispered.

A soft rumble of his chest and he kissed her again. "Yeah, probably. It's a cute ass, too tempting to ignore. And you'll love it, even if you hate it—probably more if you do."

The urge to argue the point was there, but the need to sleep won, and before she could remind him that he was supposed to be an asshole, not so damn nice and comforting, she drifted away.

CHAPTER TWELVE

Devin slid off the bed, not happy about having to leave her, and headed upstairs. Before he disappeared up the stairs he took one more look at his sleeping pet. Peaceful. For the first time since he'd snagged her, she looked peaceful while she slept. No worried brow, no tense lips, and her shoulders were soft as she hugged his pillow to her body.

He needed to get to work. Things to do, things that couldn't wait any longer.

The insistent ring of his cell prompted him to pick up his phone. He went out to the back porch; leaning against the railing, he answered.

"Tell me you're done. Because so help me god, Michael is gonna lose his shit if she's still walking around," Jason blared into the phone.

"Yeah. It's done. Well, done enough. I have what we needed." Devin turned around, shading his face from the warm sun beating down on him. The hose from the other morning still laid in the grass near the tree he had Kara tied up to. He hadn't put it away yet. The bucket with the soap was still out there. The strap he'd taken inside with him, hung it in the pantry in case he needed it again while she was inside the house.

"The girl gone?"

"Not yet. She doesn't know anything. She doesn't pose a threat to any of us."

"Not even you? You just fucking kidnapped her, and hopefully have been having a good time with the bitch." Jason laughed into the phone. If only fists could travel the same way as cellular waves, Jason wouldn't have any fucking teeth left after the phone call.

"I'm not worried." But Michael should be, they all should be. Kara, too, but she didn't fully understand that, and he wanted to keep her in the dark for just a little longer. As long as she understood that she was in danger, he could protect her from the why of it. At least for a bit more.

"Well, Michael wants her gone. Have your fun and be done with her. He wants you back in the city in two days. Has some another job for you or some shit."

"Yeah? Okay, two days. Got it. I'll just wrap it up here and get back home."

"Where'd you take her anyway?"

"An old cabin of my uncle's. No one in the family uses it no more, been falling apart for years. But hey, the cheese is good up here in Wisconsin." Better to send him north if he was going to start looking for them. If they were to show up at the farmhouse, he wasn't completely confident he could protect Kara. One of him and several of them wouldn't normally unsettle him, but Kara would add more variable. And there were too many places in the woods surrounding them for more of the Cardone family to hide.

"Fuck that state. Get back home. Michael isn't gonna want to wait any longer. He'll be back from his little vacation when you get here."

"Yeah. I got you. See you in two days." Devin clicked off the call and left his phone on the railing. Two days. More time than he could have hoped for after having already being gone for so many. It should have been a quick job: get her, get the box, get rid of her, and get home. But because she was a woman, a fucking beautiful woman, Michael was being generous letting him have some fun with her first. Kara couldn't understand how lucky she was that he managed to get the job of getting to her before someone else on the crew did. Because no fucking way Tony or any of those other assholes would have just let her off with a spanking after the shit she pulled. She'd have lost more than her pride. *Yeah, you're a real fucking saint.*

He still had two days to figure out his next move. Snagging his phone, he went up to his bedroom for a hot shower and change of clothes. Then he started making his calls, and figuring out strategy and a way out of the whole shit hole he'd found himself. Those tapes were the first thing to deal with. Even though he wasn't implicated with any actual illegal activity, he was on them talking with Tommy. The fucking idiot was playing both ways, and that was dangerous. Too fucking dangerous.

•••••••

Kara stretched out her body in the bed, her hands roaming under the pillows and feeling the cool touch of the sheets beneath her. Sheets. A bed. She was in a bed. The memory of where she was and how she got there flooded her mind and she sat up with a start. Looking around, she could see Devin had left her alone in the basement.

Not in her cage, but in the bed. The thing he'd said to her, about her wanting to be under his control, or at least a man's control. She fought it but loved it at the same time. She'd been too tired to really argue with him at the time, but would she have had much of an argument even if she was fully awake? Hadn't she been spending more and more time online looking at that exact thing? Being used, objectified, owned by someone who would take care of her and love her? But he hadn't talked about love. No, he talked about obedience and protection, but not love.

The idea that Devin could ever even possess the emotion toward someone should have made her laugh, but instead, it weighed on her that he wasn't capable of it, and what made the matter worse, he would never feel it for her.

Nothing was making any sense any more. Why should she care if he could love her? He was her captor! Kidnapper. He'd taken a belt and a strap to her ass, and then he toyed with her as if she were some pet—hell, he'd even called her a pet. Why would she want his love, and more important, why did she regret waking up in his bed alone?

So he understood a part of her that she'd hidden away and tried to ignore; that didn't mean anything at all. It just meant that she was obviously way more fucked up than she'd originally thought when she started doing all her little searches and video watching. If she had this in common with Devin, she really was in need of some help.

She scooted herself to the edge of the bed and listened for movement. If he was in the kitchen he wasn't walking around. Hopping off the bed, she padded to the stairs; still no sound and the door was open.

Needing to use the washroom, she decided it worth the risk of going upstairs without him. He'd left the door open after all and hadn't tied her up. That had to be permission in his world, right?

When she got upstairs the kitchen was empty. The bottle of oil no longer sat on the table, but she didn't need it to remind her of what he'd done. Of what she had enjoyed him doing.

She found Devin sitting in the living room. The sun had already started to fade off behind the trees, but there was enough light cascading through the windows for her to see him sitting in a large armchair in the corner, a book sitting in his lap. The boxes were gone, and the room looked cozy.

"Hey, you're up." He smiled at her from the chair, closing the book and putting it on the shelf behind him before walking to her.

"I—the door was open."

"It's okay. If the doors are open, you can come up," he nodded. He'd showered and put more clothes on. She could smell the earthy scent of his soap. The little bit of stubble from the morning was gone, too. The jeans and t-shirt he wore shouldn't have been sexy. They were just plain clothes. No designer fabrics, just pure cotton, yet on his body they sparked her arousal. Dammit. She looked away from him, surveying the room instead of his body.

"You unpack fast."

"You've been sleeping for a few hours."

"Oh." Not used to him being so civil, she wasn't really sure what to say. The vague thought that she was standing in front of him naked crept into her mind, but she'd grown so used to it. She didn't even try to cover up.

"How's your backside?"

She chose to ignore his grin. "Fine."

"Should I check?"

She nearly tripped on the rug stepping back from him. "No. I'm fine," she said again.

He laughed. "Okay. I'll take your word this time, but I'll check next time I want to. Understand? If I tell you to bend over and touch your toes so I can see your ass, you'll do it first time I ask. Got it? Remember, we're doing a new thing here. You're going to start being my good girl, and I'm going to start giving you rewards."

"Yes, Sir." The words simply materialized. Her cheeks burned with a new embarrassment.

"That's a good girl." He reached out to her, cupping her face in his hands. "See, you can be good and I can be civil. Do you want some clothes? I'll let you put on an outfit if you promise to be good, and you promise to take them off when I tell you to, no comments or complaints."

Everything changed. The man who'd strapped her in the back yard wasn't standing in front of her anymore. No, that man was reserved for when she went against him. This man, this guy holding her and stroking her face while talking with her, didn't want to hurt her—at least not in any way that didn't give them both satisfaction.

She nodded, no longer sure of her voice. "Good." He let

go of her and went over to the chair he'd been sitting in. When he returned he held a skirt and blouse in his hands. She recognized them from her closet.

"That's a Halloween costume." She couldn't help but smile. The one Halloween she agreed to go to Julie's party, she'd gone as a schoolgirl, hoping to catch the eye of one of Julie's friends. Unfortunately, that guy had brought his own schoolgirl to the party, with narrower hips and a larger bust.

He shrugged. "No matter. Just you and me here anyway." He held out the outfit to her.

"The skirt is a little short and it's getting cold—" She stopped talking when his eyebrows lifted. They were talking casually, but he wouldn't let her disobey him. That point was still crystal clear. "It's okay, it's fine." She left him in the living room and went to the bathroom to dress. A bit absurd to go to the bathroom to cover the naked body he'd just been witness to, had been looking at for days, but she did it anyway. A little privacy, something just for her—maybe a way to preserve a shred of the dignity she seemed to be giving away to him with wicked abandon.

Once she finished buttoning the blouse, she checked her reflection. Her hair was a curly mess, no matter how many times she ran her fingers through it, and without her makeup bag, there wasn't much she could do about her face. She never prescribed to the idea of putting on her face every time she left the house, but a little mascara would have brightened her appearance a bit. Maybe give her a fresher look.

Kara started to glare at the girl in the mirror. Where the hell was her backbone? She wanted to look fresher for who? Him? Her kidnapper? Taking a deep breath, she pushed herself to stop worrying about her mental state. There would be plenty of that after she got home, and if there was any chance of that happening, she had to start giving over to Devin.

He may be an asshole when he wanted to get his point across, but in the past days she'd known him he hadn't told her a single lie. Everything he promised, he delivered, even when it meant taking that damn strap to her backside. If he said he could get them both out of the mess, she had to give him a try.

Besides, her ass wasn't looking for a rematch with that strap, and trying to run again would guarantee that.

Devin leaned against the wall outside the bathroom waiting for her when she opened the door. His eyes were darkened, not with irritation for once, but concern.

"You okay?" The softness of his voice threw her.

"What? Yeah. I just wanted a minute." She tugged on the hem of her shirt, trying desperately to make it stay down. The red and black plaid pleated skirt barely covered her ass, and the shirt didn't hide her belly button. She'd been a little thinner when she'd worn the outfit last, so she was pretty sure of the picture she made now. Though you wouldn't know it looking at him. Hungry as ever.

"You were right about that skirt." He smiled, not looking away from her face. "Guess you'll have to change again before we leave. I think I might have grabbed some pants, I'll check later."

"What about the jeans I was wearing before, can't I just put those back on?"

He ignored her and pointed to the living room as he walked away. She followed, grateful to at least be upstairs and dressed. Pushing it would be stupid. He plunked himself down on the armchair and pointed to the carpeting at his feet.

"I have to sit on the floor?" She tried not to sound irritated by the idea, but by the raised eyebrow she figured she'd failed.

"No, you have to kneel on the floor. You'll sit when you learn not to question me like that. Really, peaches, I'd think you'd have that tone of yours under control by now." The mock disappointment sent a flare of anger through her, but she wouldn't give him the satisfaction of seeing it. No, he would just throw her over his lap and spank her, or stick his fingers up her ass again, or bring her back down to the cage, so she wouldn't let him win.

Sinking to her knees facing him, she placed her palms down on her knees and kept her eyes level with his.

"See, you can be good. I like it when you're good, peaches." He ran a single finger along her temple, gathering a loose strand of hair and tucking it behind her ear. "Now. I've listened to all the tapes, and have a better idea of what we're dealing with. Michael wants you dead. He doesn't care if you promise to stay quiet, if you move to Canada, doesn't matter. He wants you dead."

Her body trembled; dead. Hadn't he been telling her that the whole time? "You aren't going to kill me." She kept her voice even, though it took all of her strength to do it.

His gaze flickered away for a split second before returning to her. "No. I'm not." His tongue ran along his teeth before he continued to explain. "Here's what's going to happen. I have a friend in the city, someone who can keep you safe while I finish this mess up with Michael."

"Can't I just stay here?" Going back to Chicago didn't hold much appeal anymore.

"No. If something goes wrong, you'd be all alone up here. Only Trevor knows where this place is and he's off on a case. You'll be safe with Blake. You won't give him any trouble, either. You won't try to leave his place, and you won't try to wiggle him into helping you run away, do you understand me?" The force with which he said the words sent goosebumps over her skin.

"I don't need a babysitter, Devin."

He laughed. "Like hell you don't. It's as much for your protection as to keep you where I put you."

"Trevor's a cop, can't he just take care it? Can't he arrest Michael and his guys?"

Devin shook his head. "Doesn't work that way, peaches."

"Maybe I can help you." She leapt up onto her knees, her ass no longer resting on her feet.

"How can you help me?"

"I don't know, but I'm sure you'll need help. Maybe I can talk to Michael, or distract him, or do something while you do something else." She sounded like a little kid begging to go to the mall.

His grin should have surprised her; his soft chuckle did. "You still don't get it, peaches. I'm helping *you*. I'm saving *your* ass. You are just going to have to let me handle this. You are just going to have to stay with Blake, and be a good girl for me and do what I tell you to."

"I'm not some little kid, Devin. I can take care of myself." The pout she heard in her own voice wasn't lost on her, but she hoped he didn't hear it, or at least wouldn't remark on it. Giving in to him was getting easier to do, but she didn't have to enjoy it.

He leaned forward, grasping her chin between two fingers and pinching hard. "I never said you were a little kid. I know you can take care of yourself, it's one of the things I—" He clamped his mouth shut and shook his head before he finished his thought. "Sometimes, you can't. Sometimes you have to lean on someone else, someone a little bigger and a little stronger. There's no shame in that. Not everything in the fucking world is your responsibility, Kara."

Her breath hitched, and she felt the taste of her comeback simmering in her mouth, but she remained silent. This was his lesson. This was the thing he wanted her to learn. She needed him, but she had already learned that. Out of all the people who came and went in her life, she felt in her core that she could lean on Devin. If he said he'd catch her, he would. And damn her for wanting him to be her safety net.

"Okay."

"Good." He placed a quick kiss to the tip of her nose and sat back. "Now, tomorrow morning we'll leave after breakfast. I'll take you to Blake and he'll keep you safe. But you have to listen to him Kara, just like if he were me. If you don't, he has just as heavy a hand as I do, and he won't think twice about applying it to your naughty ass. Then he'll tie you up until I get back. So if I were you, I'd really think twice before doing something you shouldn't."

"I think you have some very dark friends, Devin." She'd meant it as a joke, but he didn't smile.

"You have to listen to him, do what he says. If he says go, you go, if he says hide, you fucking hide. And if you don't, if he has to take you in hand, I promise you it will be double worse when I get my hands on you." As a threat, it held promise. But it wouldn't be necessary. Devin was doing everything to help her, to protect her; she'd follow his instructions. She'd obey.

"Your ape of a friend will be there, how could I possibly get into trouble," she huffed. Never setting eyes on Blake, she couldn't be sure of his size, but considering how Devin looked, she assumed his friend be just the same.

He laughed. "By trying to help me. If you so much as take one step out his door without Blake knowing about it, his belt and your ass are going to get real intimate."

"I thought I was your pet? You'd let your friend do that?" It hadn't occurred to her until that moment that someone else may take Devin's place. That after all the mess and tears, she'd have to give him up for someone else. The idea made her stomach turn.

Again his lips curled up into a smile, a sexy, heated grin that made her lick her lips in anticipation of his kiss. Though it never came. "Make no mistake, you are my pet. He won't touch you other than to punish you. No one will ever touch you the way I do, not ever again. You are mine, pet. No one else's."

The soft hammering in her chest was a warning. He was close, closer than she'd let anyone get in a long time. He'd wiggle his way all the way in if she didn't start being more careful.

"When this is all over, I'll go home. You'll have to get a new pet." She tried to twist her lips into a mocking smile, but her heart wasn't fully invested. Instead, the reminder that her time with him was coming to an end darkened her mood. That moment, of her kneeling at his feet, talking, sharing a playful banter, it was good. A peaceful moment among days of chaos and fear.

"Don't get too far ahead of yourself there, pet. I may not let you off your leash, even after the coast is all clear."

His proclamation should have settled her nerves, but it missed the mark. The collar around her throat tightened, though he hadn't moved to touch it. Heavy leather pressed against her neck and reminded her he was right. He could keep her there, he could keep her forever, and who would know? And would she mind?

The low growl of her stomach interrupted the quiet moment between them. "Sorry." She placed her hands over her stomach, and he let go of her chin.

"Let's get you some food."

"What about the rest of the plan?" She moved to her feet when he signaled her to.

"That's all of it. I take you to Blake's, and you stay there, I go." He shrugged and walked away. He had a distinct walk. She hadn't noticed it earlier. More of a swagger really. The way a man who had no self-doubt would walk into a room.

CHAPTER THIRTEEN

"You're a decent cook." Kara shoveled another piece of chicken into her mouth. He watched her jaw work as she chewed the grilled meat then her throat as she swallowed.

"You don't cook?"

"For just me? No, not really. Salads, sandwiches, maybe pasta but not like this." She pointed to her near empty plate with her fork. They'd managed to get through the whole meal with casual conversation. Even with all the shit going on, she managed to actually be funny. And her smile. He couldn't compare it anything else in the world, because there wasn't anything like it out there.

"You should." He took a sip of his water, watching her as she finished eating. "I'm full." She put her fork back down on her plate.

"Clean the plate, Kara." It was the second time he'd had to tell her to finish the meal. "If you don't like the plate, I'm happy to get your bowls out for you."

She blushed. A delicate pink crept up her neck and covered her entire face. He could do just that, and her pussy would weep for it.

"Trevor's your younger brother?" She pushed the vegetables around her plate.

"Three years," he nodded.

"Didn't he have to some job to do? Isn't that why he left?"

"Yep." Devin checked his phone for the time. The sun had already disappeared for the night. The chicken had taken longer to make than he'd expected.

"And you don't think we should wait for him?"

"Nope." He pointed to her plate. "Eat."

He picked up his own plate and took it to the sink to wash. The end of a mission always brought the most stress. If everything went as planned, she'd be safe. Forever. If one thing, one tiny fucking detail didn't get taken care of, she could still be in danger. And that wouldn't sit well with him.

Blake would protect her and do what he asked of him. He had no doubts there. They'd been friends since basic training. After having just finished his last tour of duty he was taking time off, and having Devin dump Kara in his lap would at least distract him from his boredom. No way anyone could be bored with Kara around.

Watching Kara finish her dinner, he tried to forget the worry for the next day. Whatever happened he'd deal with it; so long as she was safe, it would be fine. Keeping her safe, keeping her alive, that was his new goal. Making sure she got out of the shit show of a situation so she could continue on with her life. That's what mattered now.

"You don't have a girlfriend to check in on when we get back?" She asked the question with her gaze fixed on her fork. The light pink hue deepened, but her eyes never moved.

"No. Not really the girlfriend type. Finish all of it, Kara." A clank of her plate sounded when her plate hit the table as she put it back down.

"I can see why. You're bossier than girls like," she muttered before taking another bite of the chicken.

"Bossy? Me?" He retook his seat after rinsing off his plate and tucking it into the dishwasher. "I'm not bossy, I'm the boss. See, there's a difference. When you start spouting off demands, you're being bossy. When I do it, it's because I have the authority to do so."

Several days ago she would have thrown the plate of food at him for saying something like that. But a lot had taken place. Instead of throwing anything at him, she just sighed and took another bite of her dinner.

"I'm really full, Devin." She pointed at the small pile of potatoes and chicken left.

He eyed the plate and nodded. "How do you think you should ask to be done?" No sense in letting a teaching moment pass by.

"May I be done, Sir? I'm full." The words didn't hold any bitterness or sarcasm. The woman was more at home with herself than she wanted to admit, and when he had time, he'd show her all of it. Everything about herself she'd been denying and shoving deep down inside of herself. Maybe he could let the monster inside of him out to play longer than a few sessions. Maybe they could make it real.

"Yes, you can be done. See, not so hard, right, peaches? Go rinse off the plate and put it in the washer. Then I want you downstairs, ready for bed."

"I'm not tired." She shoved away from the table, and he kept his eyes on the sway of the skirt that lifted just enough when she walked to let him have a peek at the rounded globes of her ass.

With the stealth he learned in the military, he snuck up behind her as she finished rinsing off her plate. Just as she bent over to drop it into the dishwasher, he grabbed her by the waist and spun her around. She'd gasped; surprise or fear, didn't really matter. They both hardened his dick. He was already in motion and wouldn't be deterred.

"If you aren't tired now, you will be." The promise was bold, but not untrue. Picking her up and tossing her over his shoulder, he turned for the basement.

"I'm sorry! I didn't mean to argue." She kicked her legs but he held onto her too tightly for it really to matter.

Navigating the stairs with her squirming over his

shoulder had quickly become natural for him. When they got downstairs he went to the bed and placed her back on her feet. Her bottom lip was sucked in behind her teeth and her eyes searched his. She probably thought she could make out all of his thoughts and feelings, but she'd be wrong. He made his living hiding those things where people couldn't see them.

"You're not in trouble, pet." He gave her a grin. "You've been very good today. I'm going to reward you." He started to unbutton her blouse, only having to swat one hand away when she made a half-ass attempt to block him. "Put your hands down at your sides," he instructed but didn't stop in his ministrations to see if she obeyed. He didn't need to; she would obey him.

Each small white button slid through the hole with ease, and he slipped the material over her shoulders, exposing her breasts again. He'd missed them during the day. Letting her wear clothing had been a reward for her, but torture for him. He wanted her naked, open to him at all times.

"You're trembling." His fingers brushed along her collarbone. "Would it be easier if this was a punishment?"

"No, I don't want a punishment, Sir," she said with a steady voice. She wasn't afraid. No, the tremors were from arousal, desire, and her need to be dominated by him. Uncertainty lingered in her eyes, causing the trembles, but he knew how to calm those. He also knew how to entice them.

"Good, because I'm going to redden your ass and it will be much better for you if you behave."

Her gaze moved to the wall with paddles, whips, crops, and floggers dangling from hooks. He owned a full arsenal, and he'd used every toy hanging there. All willing, all wanting women who bent over for him to do exactly what he was planning to do with Kara. His little pet. But none of them compared to the energy his pet emitted for him, to the high her submission gave him.

"I don't think it will feel good," she said, still looking at the toys with disapproval.

He gave a little laugh and cupped her breasts, tweaking her nipples to bring her attention back to him. And back to him she came, along with a sharp gasp. There was that little sound again. The beauty in just that soft melody hardened his dick to almost unbearable proportions. "I promise you, everything about right now is to make you feel good. So long as you behave; if you defy me, lie to me, disobey me, then I can't help you. What's the decision you get to make?"

He pinned her down with a stare; keeping her eyes locked with his became easier each time. She wasn't softening, no, she was finding her strength. Finding that thing inside of her that made her feel real, alive, and exactly who she really was.

"I decide to obey or disobey, Sir." Clear, precise answer that pushed a smile onto his lips.

"That's right, good girl." He wrapped his hand behind her neck and pulled her to him, their lips mashing together in a heated exchange. Every bit of passion he took from her, she gave to him now; there was no forcing or manipulation. No, when they kissed, the truth of her soul became exposed.

"Now, lift up that skirt and bend over the side of the bed for me, prop your ass up for me nice and high."

Her mouth opened, some smart-ass reply surely tingled her tongue, but with a raised eyebrow from him, she snapped it shut. He waited for her to get in position. It wasn't every day a beautiful woman bent over his bed and offered her ass to him, and he wasn't going to waste the moment with his back to her.

The cotton fabric of her skirt inched up, exposing her round ass at an unhurried pace. He couldn't help but wet his lips as she finished bunching it up around her hips. She caught his stare for a moment, held onto it then flickered away, turning to face forward. She wasn't sure he could give her pleasure with a spanking, but he'd surprised her before. He had no doubt he'd be doing it again.

A haunting question of why he wanted to give her

pleasure with a spanking loomed in his mind as he studied his tools on the wall. She wasn't his to keep, she'd be free in a few days. Odds of them making anything real out of what they've been through were damn small. He'd kept her safe, even from herself—mostly. Could she see past it all? Maybe that's why he needed to show her she could enjoy a spanking, enjoy his belt and his hand, and a paddle. If she would admit that she liked those things, that she was just as much of a masochist as he was a sadist, she'd forget about the rough way she came into his possession.

He'd never meant to strap her; it wasn't on the list of things to do. But she'd done everything opposite of what he expected, and she didn't listen. She could have hurt herself or him; no, he wouldn't regret the punishments, but he was more than that. He could offer more.

Plucking a heavy flogger from the wall, he went back to her side. The thick falls would give her a hard thuddy slap, but should she move from position, the ends could deliver a sharp bite from the devil himself.

"Keep your eyes forward, pet, I want to play." He snapped his fingers and pointed in front of her. She hesitated for a beat then looked away. "Now, hold this for me." Draping the flogger over her back, he took a moment to enjoy the sight of the black and gold falls splayed out against her creamy skin.

Focusing his attention on her ass again, he ran both hands over her unblemished backside. All the bruises and welts had faded completely. A musical hiss left her lips as he dragged his nails across her ass, spreading her cheeks. She kept her face forward, but he knew the blush was there; it had already begun to spread to her neck and her back. Fucking her in the ass would kill him, he decided. There wasn't time to train her well enough to make sure she enjoyed it as much as him. No, he'd save that for later. If a bastard like him was lucky enough to be granted a future.

With a steady hand, he delivered a few test swats to her ass, delighting in the soft jiggle of her flesh with each spank.

She barely made a sound. He went harder. Still just a hushed breath, so he went harder. One hard slap to her thighs and she yelped, pushing her torso off the bed. "Nuh-uh, none of that now. You stay down until I tell you to move. I can tie you down if you want." He wanted, but he'd give her that call.

"I'll hold still." Her body jostled as she readjusted her stance; the flogger slipped a hair but remained on her back.

Placing his hand flat on her back, he let half a dozen swats fall in rapid fire with hardened force. A little wiggle of her hips and a groan from her lips, but otherwise she remained still. Her ass was quickly turning a nice shade of pink. Six more slaps to her other cheek. Symmetry meant a lot to him.

Her groan amplified when he moved to her thighs, but she didn't kick out, or ask him to stop. Not that he would have. Not yet, not when he was just beginning to get a whiff of her arousal.

Taking a break, he pulled her ass cheeks apart again. "Open your legs a bit, pet," he ordered and waited for her to wiggle her feet apart before slicing his fingers through her folds, gathering up the influx of juices there. Her ass pushed out further for him, taking his two fingers into her passage like a good little slut. He shook his head. She wasn't his. This was just for fun. He couldn't be using those words to describe her or he'd never let her go.

He thrust his fingers in and out of her with his left hand and peppered her ass with his right. The moans and groans all melted together, and he wasn't sure if she was making sounds from the slap or his fingers.

"That's enough of that," he chided her, wiping his wet fingers across her ass. Her head bowed forward.

•••••••

The flogger dragged across her back as he removed it. Kara could feel the heat in her ass almost as much as the heat in her pussy. The instruction to close her legs hadn't come, and she was too eager to have her reward to disobey him now.

Whatever part of her mind that worked to tell her she was in a bad situation, that she should run back into her cage and lock the door, wasn't working. Instead, she pressed her chest further against the plush bedding and stuck her ass further into the air.

Just an experiment, she told herself. She'd fantasized about this, a powerful, sexy man holding a flogger in his hand with her ass upturned in front of him. Orgasms abounded with that image in her head for years, and now she had the real thing. She would have to ignore the fact that she hated him. She could do that, separate herself from her feelings. Only at that moment, and the moments during the day, she didn't hate him. Hadn't hated him for a while.

She was going to need a very good shrink when this was all over.

"If it's too much, really too much, and I'll know if you're bullshitting me, you say so. Got it? If you lie, though, and I know your tolerance, there'll be more for lying. Got me?"

The light trace of his fingers on her already warmed ass might as well have been a stroke to her clit. The place she really needed him to touch. If he would just move his hand a little lower. A sharp slap to her ass stilled her thoughts.

"No humping the fucking bed, pet!" Another sharp slap upward, onto her pussy. Had she been grinding against the bedding? She was worse off than she thought. "Now, do you understand?"

"Yes," she nodded and another sharp slap to her ass reminded her of her manners. "Sir! Yes, Sir."

"Good." In her mind she could almost see him nod with a satisfied grin. He ran his hand down both thighs, rubbing away the sting of his slaps.

The first fall of the flogger surprised her. It hurt, but not overly much, nothing like the strap and not even as much as his hand. There was no sting to it, only a thick thud. Again it crossed her ass, and then again. The warmth of the implement began to build, and she started to feel the effects compiling on top of each stroke, settling her into a comfortable heat. And then he unleashed hell on her. The very tips of the flogger grazed her ass and she yelped, nearly launching off the bed. "Stay," he commanded with a harsh voice. Again he struck her, higher, and with just as much of a pinpoint sting.

"Fuck!" She stomped one foot as he did it again, lower this time. He seemed to be making his way over her entire ass.

"You can cuss, but keep that foot down. I said not to get out of position." She clenched her teeth and thought of several things to say to him, but the next strike across her thighs wiped her mind clean.

"Ah!" Her foot managed to stay planted, but she threw her head back and took a deep breath. More strikes with the flat of the falls, luring her into a safe place that held no actual safety. Not for her. Not with him holding the damn flogger.

She heard the rustling of clothes behind her and wondered if he was stripping. Would she see him nude if she looked over her shoulder, and would he punish her for looking?

Another swat with the flogger and her attention snapped right back to the heat building between her legs. As though he knew her thoughts, he swung upward, catching her pussy with the falls.

"Spread those legs," he ordered and damn her if she didn't just go right ahead and do exactly as he said. The flogger hit her pussy again, clipping her clit. The pain shot right through her body, making her tremble. Need. She was so fucking needy at that moment, and he just kept making it worse with the flogger, and then his hand. Two fingers dove into her pussy, and like the slut he'd turned her into, she arched her back and took him as fully as she could.

Her back became his next target, but she relished each strike. Each sharp bite of the tips, coupled with the strokes of his fingers. A fog crept around her, muddling her thoughts. Her body absorbed the impact of the flogger, her mind craved the next one before the last was given.

The blows got harder, stronger, his fingers fucked her with more force. She clasped her hands together to keep from reaching back, not to shield herself, but to grasp for him. His touch was what she craved.

A harder lash across her back brought her torso off the bed again, but she didn't turn, didn't try to stand. The flogger appeared beside her on the bed, his mouth locked on her back, teeth biting into her flesh, his tongue sweeping over the tenderized flesh. She hissed, writhed beneath the assault but moved further toward him, offering herself to him.

Her body tensed, ready to explode, just needing a few more strokes, just the right touch. Preparing for her orgasm, she tightened her legs, arched higher, breathed heavier. Wanting nothing more at that moment than to feel her clit shoot off the fireworks she knew it would.

He moved his hand. The fucker took his hand away and stopped the flogging. "Nuh-uh. Not yet." He gently patted her ass. Turning to glare at him over her shoulder, she felt a response coming, something stinging that would put him in as much discomfort as her, but his satisfied smile stopped her.

"What? You didn't think it'd be that easy, did you?" He patted the lower curve of her ass again. The settled burn ignited with his touch, though she doubted she needed a spank to reignite that fire. Just his touch would have worked fine.

"I'm glad you're having so much fun," she snorted and turned forward again. Why had she thought he'd be easy on her, let her have little fun, too?

The leather strap around her neck was yanked backward, pulling her up to her feet. "Don't think that because we are having some play time, that you can use that mouth of yours to be disrespectful, pet."

He didn't move, just stood beside her with his hands dangling at his sides. Why didn't he say something or do something? Waiting. He waited for something. Her mind rebelled, but she couldn't help what her heart knew. She had been disrespectful. The pleasure he was giving her was a reward, and when he didn't give her exactly what she wanted, she'd rolled her eyes like a spoiled brat. He was waiting for exactly the thing she didn't want to do, but would. Not because she ached so much for her release, but because she cared if he was displeased with her.

Seeing his irritation and disappointment aimed at her hurt. Not like his belt, or his strap, but somewhere inside. Deep inside of her, ached when she did wrong.

"I'm sorry," she whispered. "Sir. I'm sorry, Sir." Without looking at him, unable to look up at his eyes, because his eyes would see things she didn't want to share. Not yet. Not when she was only just finding this place inside of her for herself. She sank to her knees in front of him. She put her hands on her thighs, palms down, and her head bowed. Waiting for what came next. It was play time, a reward for being so good; had she fucked it all up with one movement? One stupid moment of rebellion?

His hand rested on the top of her head, and on pure instinct she leaned into him. Her face pressed against his leg, into the fabric of his pants while his hand remained steady in place. She closed her eyes, not to keep from seeing, but to let herself feel the awesome sense of relief that washed over her at his touch. Without a single word, he'd bridged the gap she'd put between them.

Maybe it was wrong. Maybe she should have fought harder against what was happening to her because of what and who he was, but it was too late. The feelings, the emotional connection, the desires and the hopes were all mingled together, and all of them revolved around him.

"Up, pet." He lifted her to her feet and captured her face between his hands, holding her exactly where he wanted her. His eyes met hers, searching and exploring the depths of her that she wanted so desperately to hide. Not just from him, but from herself. She'd known about her fantasies, knew she was different than most woman in the sexual department, but never did she know how deeply it went.

"You make me happy." He cracked a smile, small, just a little lift of his lips, but still a smile. "Lie on your back now, I want to see your pussy."

Moving onto the bed, she rolled over onto her back. He gripped her ankles and dragged her ass to the edge of the bed. "Keep your feet planted, and your legs spread for me. Don't close them. Got me?"

"Yes, Sir," she nodded, and tried to relax her hands at her sides. He picked up the flogger again and swished the falls in front of him while staring at her. No one ever stared at her down there, and she hadn't been able to shave in the past few days. Embarrassed, she turned her head to the side, not wanting to see if his desire turned to disgust.

"Look at me, pet," he snapped, only continuing once she was again facing him. "You have the prettiest pussy I've ever seen." His words were spoken in a soft voice, and even softer fingers touched her, sending an electrifying energy through her body. Before she could respond, he leaned down, flogger in one hand, her pussy beneath the other, and licked her from her entrance all the way up to her clit.

She sucked in her breath, willing herself to keep her hips planted on the bed. A sharp nibble to her clit made her resolve crumble, and she arched upward. He chuckled against her clit, but continued his playful biting. When he was finished there, he went back to licking and sucking at her lips. His fingers moved lower, toying with her entrance as he continued to torture her clit. He wouldn't let her come, not yet, but she still tried to get to that release before he could stop her. Except he was a master at knowing her body, and as she rounded the bend, going head first toward that release, he stepped back again, wiping the back of his hand across his mouth with a wide sadistic grin. The bastard!

"Now, hold still. Do not close those pretty legs of yours

or your ass will take the punishment. I have a nice set of plugs that would do nicely, but you aren't really ready for them yet so it would be a shame if I had to use one before then. Again, whose choice is it?" He took a few practice swings with the flogger, never taking his gaze off of her. "Pet?"

"Mine, Sir." She exhaled and flopped her head back on the mattress.

"What choice do you have?" he asked again, sounding more like a teacher going over study notes than a man holding a flogger above her exposed and extremely wet pussy.

"To obey, or disobey," she whispered, watching the falls of the flogger and worrying over how much pain it would cause her pussy. Worried, but not fearful. He wouldn't give her more than she could bear, and he wouldn't give her anything less than he wanted.

"Excellent. Then we can begin." Begin? What had they been doing already?

With practiced skill he brought the flogger down on her, the tips of the falls landing just above her clit, sending a shockwave of sensations through her body. Again it fell, this time to her inner thigh, then the other, before landing back on her clit. She cried out as the sharpness ran through her, but he gave her no reprieve; he struck higher, crossing over on her abdomen. He moved about, to one side of her then the other, spreading out the blows across her stomach, her breasts, before going back to her pussy.

She wiggled a bit, but otherwise she concentrated on him, on the sensations he was giving her. A heavy thud across her stomach had her wincing, but the warmth that exploded within her traveled up her body, seeping into her mind.

"Turn over, pet. I want you to grab the mattress over your head, and keep your legs straight down."

Quickly, she scurried into position, not wanting the heat from the flogger to cool. It was different than the whipping he'd given her. It hurt like fire being spread across her body, but it wasn't pain. Not mind-blowing agony, but a heated ache that crescendoed with each strike.

The falls landed over her shoulders, the sting pulling a yelp from her lips. She turned her face away from him. Again he hit her, making his way down her body, over her ass, down her legs, not even leaving her feet untouched. Her mind began to fog, to feel things outside of herself.

She could hear the flogger land, felt the pain of it, the harshness of the blows. He wasn't going easy; in fact, it seemed to be getting harder, but she wanted it, craved and welcomed each and every strike. Her eyes fixated on the wall, where a set of rings were mounted. Another blow, low on her ass, sharper, jostled her mind into focus, but quickly gave way to the pleasure of the next strike across her shoulders. She was being bathed in pain and glorious pleasure and her mind swam through it.

"Good girl," she heard him say, though he seemed a bit in the distance. When his hand touched her, she centered on him, focused only on his flesh touching hers. He dragged his nails down her back, giving her another sharp sensation to cling to. She gasped, throwing her head back and relishing in the bite of his nails. A soft pat to her ass and then a smack to her thighs. She sucked in air, not having expected the slap, then another and another. Again her mind flew further away, and she moaned. The kiss of his lips to her clit could not have compared to the touch of his palm on her ass at that moment.

A hand dove into her hair, pulling her head back. Dark eyes searched hers. "Fuck, you are more than I could have hoped for, pet." His words drifted between them, and she tried to grasp onto them, but she was too far away. Floating over them, basking in the heated ache of her body.

He kissed her. Not a mere pressing of lips together, but a taking, a claiming. Unlike the other possessive kisses he'd given her, this kiss held permanency. It wasn't a moment of possession but a change of course.

When he pulled away, she moved her eyes to his lips, wanting more from him. Wanting all of him. He patted her head and moved back around her. Her ankles were pulled backward, and she found herself with her feet on the floor and her body bent over the bed.

Wiggling her ass at him, she spread her legs, arching upward toward him. She wanted more, all of it. The head of his cock pressed against her entrance, and she didn't wait for his permission or his movement; she pushed back, impaling herself on him and groaning out loud with the pleasure.

He slapped her ass, snapping her out of her actions, and pinned her hips to the bed. "I know what you want, but you won't take it, do you understand, pet? You will not just take."

She nodded, unable to make words come to her mouth. She gripped the blankets and waited, and waited. Just when she was going to move, to look for him, he pulled out and shoved himself back into her. She cried out at the harsh thrust of his cock, but he didn't stop.

It was as if he'd seen the fire building in her and was working tirelessly to extinguish it. She lifted her right leg, hooking it on the bed, and he growled.

"Fuck. So fucking tight." He slapped her thigh, but didn't move her leg back down. Much fuller with this position, she threw her head back and cried.

Tears, real tears trickled down her cheeks as he fucked her harder and harder still. The line, the little chalk-drawn line where pain ended and pleasure began was erased with each thrust.

"Fuck! Please!" she yelled out into the room. "I have to come. Please. Please." She sucked in air while she tried to speak. Her eyes clenched on their own; there would be no stopping the orgasm that was barreling down on her.

"Yes. Pet. Come for me. Come." He slapped her again, and again. Spanks to her ass, her thigh while he pummeled harder into her passage, driving her right over the edge.

She screamed out incoherent words as her body detonated. Bucking back at him, she took every stroke he gave, and when she heard him grunting behind her, she shoved even harder at him. The waves were endless, over and over again her pussy convulsed and tensed, and released again. It was angelic torture, and by the end of it, by the time he had dug his nails into her hips and found his own release, she was plastered to the bed in a puddle.

Vaguely she heard him move, felt his cock slip from her body. A drawer opened and closed. Water ran softly from somewhere behind her. A cool cloth pressed against her pussy, wiping and soothing the delicate burn from the frantic fucking.

"Baby, you there?" Another cool washcloth ran down her back, easing some of the sting from the flogging. Muscles ached, and she couldn't focus. "Ah, there you are." His eyes were back on hers, and she tried to smile, to signal she was fine. At least she thought she was. Everything moved in a haze, the aches and stings, all of it made her want to smile and wrap herself in them. He smoothed back her hair. "Come on. Let's get you under the covers."

More movements; he helped her put her leg back down and picked her up in his arms, cradling her. He didn't lay her on the bed. He carried her upstairs. Then more stairs. Not looking at her surroundings, she tucked her head under his chin and pressed against the safety of his body. She snuggled further, breathing him in.

When he finally did lay her down, she recognized the room. His room. He'd brought her back to his bed. Soft blankets covered her, and he laid beside her, stroking her cheeks. The tears had dried, but he kissed them away anyway.

He dragged her into his arms, letting her rest her head on his chest. "Just rest, baby. Everything's going to be okay. I promise."

CHAPTER FOURTEEN

Nothing changed except for everything had. Devin sat on his bed watching his pet sleep. So fragile, yet stronger than many of the soldiers he'd fought beside. They'd gone into battle with armor and weapons; his pet had survived through sheer will and determination.

He'd already spoken to Blake and had everything set and ready to go when they got there. Kara wouldn't understand, and she would have to fall back on her spirit again. No armor. No weapons. Not for his pet.

"I am such a fucking asshole," he whispered while reaching over to stroke her cheek. One thick curl lay over her eyes, and he tucked it away, wanting to see all of her features.

The sun started to creep into the room through the blinds, but she didn't stir. It was time to make the call, get the ball rolling. He left her in the bed and tried to ignore the sour twist in his stomach.

It was early, but Jason would be awake. The man ran five miles every morning before the sun came up. He picked up on the first ring, and Devin clutched his phone to his ear, his heart starting to pound. Getting Jason to accept his proposal was the easy part; the hard sell would be the call he made next.

"Hey. I'm coming into the city this afternoon. I want a sit down. Around three."

"I'll call Michael—"

"No Michael. Just you." Devin walked down the stairs away from where Kara slept, unaware of all the dangers he was bringing down on her that day.

Jason hesitated. Devin heard his slow deep breathing through the phone before he answered. "Okay. Three. Meet me at the club." Jason owned a strip club in Lincoln Park.

"Sounds good." Devin stared up the stairs. She was still sleeping in his bed. Peaceful and completely unaware her world was about to come crashing down. "Three at the club."

"That girl problem solved?"

"Yeah, not an issue." Mostly the truth. Blake would take care of her. She'd be safe. So why the fuck was his chest so twisted up?

"Good. Michael's getting antsy." Michael was always antsy when it came to business. He wanted shit handled right away, because he couldn't be patient. Too many sloppy moves happened because of his impatience and his paranoia.

"See you at three." Devin disconnected the call and went about making the rest of them. It wasn't going to be easy; a lot was riding on the next call he made. If he couldn't get the go ahead, he'd have to keep Kara hidden for longer. Not a horrible idea, but not plausible. Not for her, and not for him.

•••••••

An hour later, the bed creaked with Kara's movement. Devin looked up at her from where he sat in the armchair. She sighed, a content sound he tried to memorize. Slender arms reached over her head as she stretched just before she opened her eyes.

"Hey," she smiled. The most brilliant sunshine smile he'd seen on her beautiful lips since he'd met her.

Nothing good was going to happen for her that afternoon, and he took all the blame. His stomach twisted again, a sour feeling he hadn't entertained since his first few years in the military. That sinking feeling of gloom and doom just before he drove off into the unknown.

"Hey, peaches." He tried to sound light, but she'd come to know him as much as he'd taught her over their time together.

"What's wrong?" She sat up, running one hand through her hair and the other lifting the sheet to cover her naked breasts.

"Nothing. You needed sleep, but it's getting late." He slapped his knees and pushed off the chair. "So, jump in the shower and get dressed. I want to be on the road within the hour."

"Um. Okay." She pulled her knees up to her chin. "Are you sure Blake is okay with me going there? I mean he doesn't know me, and—"

"Don't worry about the details, just get ready to go." He pulled the top drawer of his dresser open and pulled out the bag with her clothes in it. "Here." He dropped it on the bed. Giving her a quick glance, he sat on the bed. "You're sore today." He didn't need to ask. It had been a hard session; when he realized how quickly she started to fly from the flogger, he'd given her more and more. There would probably be a mark or two on her body as well.

"Just a little." Her cheeks flushed. "I was really tired after, huh?" She scratched the back of her neck.

"You were flying a little high from the flogging." He put his hand on her knee, feeling the warmth of her to remind him of what he was fighting for, why he was walking head first into the fire.

"Flying? That's what it felt like, yeah."

"It's called subspace. Not everyone gets there."

She nodded. She probably had heard the term before.

He'd have to figure out what to do for her when it all ended. She couldn't just be dropped off and left on her own. She needed someone to show her the way, otherwise she'd end up getting some asshole to take her under his wing. That thought, the image of another man holding a flogger or paddle or belt over her made his blood pound in his ears, and he didn't need the distraction. Not then. Not when they were both so close to getting out of the mess her brother had neatly put them in.

"Do you want to see?" The question came out so hushed, he barely heard her. She wasn't looking at him either, just staring off toward the bathroom.

"See what? Your body?" His dick hardened at the thought. "Yeah. Stand up." One last look. He could handle that.

She slid from the bed, leaving the sheet behind. Her pupils were already dilated, and if he touched her pussy, he would bet his life savings that he'd find her wet and warm for him.

"Put your hands behind her back, yeah, like that." He stood from the bed, taking in the beauty before him. Her breasts, so heavy in his hands, hung with pride from her body, her nipples peaked under his scrutiny, and goosebumps covered her skin.

No bruising on her breasts or stomach. Good. He'd been careful, but she'd taken to the heaviness of the flogger so well, he'd also gone a little heavier than he planned. "Turn around." She didn't argue, or even look at him; she just moved her feet until her ass was facing him. A few small bruises on her ass, nothing that would last long, or give her any trouble after a day or so.

She looked over her shoulder at him, licked her lips, and smiled. "Do you want to, you know… Get a closer look?" The tease was there, the offering of her body to him. The girl wanted more of what he'd given.

He pulled back. "Not now. Get in the shower, peaches. Here. Let's take this off." He brushed her hair away from the back of her neck and unbuckled the leather collar. Slipping it off of her, he held it in his hands. The weight of the leather seemed greater.

With graceful steps she turned back to face him. "What's wrong?" she asked again, her hand resting on his forearm.

He looked from the collar to her face and stepped away. "Nothing. Shower and get dressed." He clamped his hand around the strip of leather and walked out of the room.

Pained eyes followed him out, and as he closed the bedroom door, he didn't miss the longing in her eyes when she watched him shove her collar in his pocket. She wouldn't be getting it back, and she knew it. Why the fuck did it bother him so much that she didn't like that idea? He didn't like it either. Fuck. "Shower!" he yelled through the closed door then stomped downstairs to finish putting everything together. One more call to the field office to be sure the teams were all in place for the takedowns, and they could get on the road.

•••••••

Something changed. Devin sat beside her in his truck, driving in complete silence. He was brooding, but she didn't understand why. She hadn't argued with him at all, not when he ordered her to eat the oatmeal she hated, not when he still refused to give her her phone back, and not a peep when he told her to get in the car and sent her on her way with a hard slap to her ass.

He'd rejected her in the bedroom, and taken her collar. When she went downstairs, she checked to see if it was still in his pocket, ready to be put back in place. It wasn't there. She wanted to ask him for it, had even opened her mouth to let the words tumble out. But then he'd pointed to her untouched oatmeal and told her to her eat, or he'd do it for her. She hadn't heard his tone harden like that since she'd tried to escape him the first time.

She wasn't trying to escape anymore. The exact opposite

now, she wanted to stay. Couldn't they just stay in the farmhouse? Surely, he could go back to the city on his own, finish whatever he needed to finish then just come back to the house. He'd said it was his retirement. That had to mean he was almost ready to do just that.

Signs for Chicago started popping up with more regularity as they drove. Her stomach cramped. "Devin, what's going to happen?"

"I told you. You're going to Blake's, and when I get back—" He looked over his shoulder and merged into the right lane. "When I get back this will be over."

"Then what? I go home?" Her mouth dried at the question. She didn't want to go home. Not alone.

"Everything is going to be okay, Kara." He didn't look at her when he said the words, though. He hadn't looked at her since they got in the truck several hours ago. And the only time he talked to her was to ask if she needed to pee.

"That's not what I asked you," she demanded. Enough of the silence and the pouting, and the misplaced anger. "I asked you what exactly is going to fucking happen."

"Watch yourself, peaches. I still have my belt, and you still have your ass." A smirk crossed his lips, but still he didn't look at her.

Deciding it best not to test him, she crossed her arms over her chest and looked out the window. Familiar landscapes came into view as they grew closer to the city.

Any further attempts at a conversation with Devin went unnoticed. In a few hours she'd be free of him. The thought should have made her happy. Elated! Instead, the world was crumbling around her again. She'd be back to being all alone. Except this time, for the first time since her mother died, it felt like a black curtain was starting to fall over her. Alone meant no Devin. It meant she'd be on her own. She could do that, but she didn't want to. Not anymore. Not after sleeping in his arms, kneeling at his feet, eating from his hands. No. She didn't want to be alone anymore. She wanted to curl up inside of him and let him shelter her, protect her, and love her.

Love. He never mentioned love. His actions did though. She rubbed her temples. Thoughts like that were going to get her heart broken. He didn't love her. He did what he thought he needed to do. He protected her, and he would keep doing that until this was finished. But what then? Did they exchange phone numbers? Go for coffee? What was going to happen then?

As the car pulled off the expressway and mingled with the other cars in the clogged street of the city, her muscles tightened. A dull ache in her chest grew.

"Just a few minutes more." He pulled out his cell phone and started dialing. She looked behind them again. Parked cars, cars driving at the normal limit. The porches of the buildings they passed were empty. "Hey. It's me. The pet is on the leash."

Who the hell was he talking to? Pet? Her? He referred to her that way to everyone? "Ten minutes out."

After he clicked off the call she glared at him. "Pet? Were you talking about me?"

He gave her a smile, one of his cocky grins that suggested she'd gone as far as he would allow. "Don't get your panties in a wad." He went back to watching the road and she went back to steaming. The asshole. After last night she thought things had changed. He'd been so soothing, so powerful. He'd given her everything she'd ever wanted, and then morning came, and he ripped it all away. She'd wait until after this little meeting, then they'd talk. She'd get her answers. Everything was going to be okay. He'd promised.

Devin parked behind a garage in an alley. "Here we are." He sighed and turned off the ignition, but made no move to get out of the truck. "Listen. Kara. You have to stay safe, and the only way for that to happen is with Blake. You do everything he says, even if you don't understand why, okay?" There was something so raw, so naked in his voice, her heart started to pound.

"I already promised to be a good girl." She tried to force

a lightness to her words, though nothing felt light between them anymore.

He looked at her. Really looked at her. His brow wrinkled with concern, his eyes drooped with something close to guilt. The truth hit her, or started to sink in. She'd known it before, but she tried to deflect it.

"You are coming back for me, right?" The desperation in her voice couldn't be controlled, and she really hated that she couldn't hide her emotions better.

He frowned. "Blake will take care of you. He's a good guy."

Before she could point out that he hadn't answered her question, his door opened and he jumped out. He stood at the front of the truck waving her to follow. She grabbed her purse—he'd left it in the truck with her—and hopped out.

CHAPTER FIFTEEN

Devin parked his truck in the back lot of the strip club. The neon sign of a dancer blinked overhead, but with the sun still hanging in the sky the lighting didn't show so well.

The thudding of music from outside the room filtered in, and the thick scent of cigars hung in the air when Devin walked into the back room of the club.

Around a small poker table sat three men. Everyone dressed in finer suits than he'd ever own. Silk ties? No one was smoking, but gray smoke from a previously lit cigar hung stagnant in the air over the table.

All three looked up from the table, but only one tensed at the sight of him walking in. The younger of the three, his jaw tightened and his knuckles whitened as he clenched his cards.

"Hey, Dev!" The other two waved a hand in the air with pleasant smiles. "'Bout time you got back."

"I need a minute with Jason, fellas."

The men looked to their boss, who gave a flip of his head toward the back door. Chairs scraped, cards dropped on the green felt, and then they were gone, only glancing once more toward Devin before disappearing into the loud music and cigarette smoke.

"What's going on, Dev?"

Devin walked up to the table, pulled out a chair, and plunked himself down.

"Michael's been worried about you." Jason's voice was thick.

"Michael worries about everyone," Devin huffed. "And to that point." Devin folded his hands on the table. "I found what Michael was afraid of. Tapes. A whole mess of them. Tommy's been recording conversations for years."

"Fuck." Jason wiped his hand over his face, taking a moment to let it sink in. "Years?"

Devin gave a little laugh. "Yeah. Years, the idiot. He sent them all up to a post office box, paid some old man to keep an eye out for the packages and to store them if his box got full."

"You listen to them?"

"Oh, yeah," Devin nodded. "Every one of them." He shuffled in his chair and pulled out an envelope from inside his coat. He opened it and dumped the dozen small cassettes onto the table. "These are the recordings of your conversations with Tommy, or any conversations where you're mentioned."

Jason picked up one of the cassettes and looked at it as though it would simply start playing in his hands. "There are others?"

"Of you? No. That's all of them. No duplicates have been made," Devin assured him, tossing the empty envelope on the table.

"What about Michael?"

"He's on his way out," Devin shrugged. Jason's eyes narrowed, and he dropped the cassette to the table.

"You have my attention."

Devin nodded and relaxed his shoulders. "Right now, Michael and his crew are being arrested." Devin put a hand out, stilling Jason's jerking movements as he started to reach into his coat. "Relax. Relax." He patted his hand. "No one's coming here. Or your house, or any of your men's houses.

Your crew is staying clean."

"My crew?" Jason leaned back in his chair. He flushed as he listened to Devin.

"Yeah. You and your crew are being left alone. The tapes with Michael or mention of Michael, they aren't here."

"You fucking rat!" Jason spit on the table.

"No rat. I had nothing to do with this shit. Those tapes, Tommy made those tapes before I even came to this crew. Now, instead of trying to shoot my head off, listen up. You're taking over your brother's kingdom. Forget this little crew shit, you have it all now. The feds aren't coming for you. They want him, and they have him. Business goes on as usual, except your pockets are getting lined with gold instead of his."

Jason licked his lips, his nostrils flared. "What the fuck is in it for you, Michael getting taken down? You want on my crew?"

Devin laughed. "I want nothing. I'm walking away and never looking back at this shitty city again. Letting you free, giving you the throne, that's my life insurance. You don't come after me."

Jason shook his head. "It's Michael you'll need to worry about."

"That's not a worry." Devin glanced at the door behind Jason, the one leading out into the club. "You'll be in charge of everything now. Starting now."

"Michael's always been afraid I'd take shit over under his nose. That paranoid fuck has been busting my balls for years, and you, one of his valued men, come in here and hand the whole business to me on a platter."

Devin sat back in his chair, moving his hands to his lap. "I can't protect anything you do after this, but from what's gone down, you're clear. Do with that what you want."

Jason eyed him silently. Michael wouldn't have hesitated; he would have pulled out his pistol and taken Devin out. But Jason was more controlled, more levelheaded. It was that part of him Devin was counting on to keep himself alive.

"What are you going to do with the girl? Michael will still have some connections; he's going to go after her if he thinks she's alive. Because this is gonna get pinned on her—and you." Jason jabbed a finger at him.

"She's protected," Devin shrugged. "My concern isn't so much for her. She's not even a player in all this, never was."

"Michael trusted you." The distaste for him was evident in Jason's tone.

"No, he didn't. And like I said. I had nothing to do with those tapes."

"They just magically appeared in the cops' lap?" Jason's eyes narrowed. Even with being handed his kingdom, a rat was a rat.

"Something like that. Tommy was stupid." Devin stood from his chair and turned on his heel.

"You think you can just walk away from shit like this? You think I don't get what happened, I don't know what you really are?"

Devin didn't turn around, he just kept walking to the exit. "I think you should take the gift being given to you. Because I promise you, this is the better deal."

He half expected Jason to pull his gun and start firing at him before he got to the door, but he made it to the truck in one piece. Aside from his heart hammering in his chest, and his breath barely coming to him with much ease, he thought he handled the situation pretty well.

• • • • • • •

Blake was nothing like Devin. Aside from the fact that he was a mammoth in comparison, and built like an ox, his personality was even harsher. Blue eyes, crystal blue eyes, watched her as she paced his living room.

The apartment was a spectacular specimen of cleanliness. Not a speck of dust could be seen anywhere. The carpet looked as though he ran the vacuum just before she arrived. Either he was a completely neat freak, or he'd done a last-minute scrub to make the place inhabitable for guests. Considering the coaster he put under her glass of water, she was leaning toward neat freak.

"You'll wear a hole in the floor if you keep it up. Sit down." Blake's deep voice interrupted the silence.

Kara ignored him and went to the window, pulling back the curtains to peer out at the street. It was a no-no, but the longer Devin was gone, the shorter her fuse was getting.

"Kara, last warning, get away from the windows and sit down." Blake didn't move from the armchair he sat in, just watching her as she walked around his pristine apartment.

"Or what? You'll pull me over your lap and give me a spanking?" she muttered, letting the curtain fall back in place and turning to glare at him.

The right side of his lips curled up, and he crossed his arms over his muscular chest. "You're a tester. Like to push the boundaries to make sure they are there?"

She eyed him cautiously. Devin had given him the go ahead to do just what she was teasing him about, and at the sight of his saucer hands, she wasn't really jumping at the idea. Besides. Her ass was Devin's to punish, not Blake's.

"I'll stay away from the window," she nodded and plopped back on the couch. She grabbed her purse from the coffee table and opened it as his phone rang. The purse had been sitting between her and Devin the whole ride back from Michigan, but she'd never opened it. Now though, she unzipped it and pulled the faux leather apart, gasping at what she saw.

Bills. Wrapped in bands. Her entire purse was full of the bundles. No wonder it had been so much heavier than she remembered.

Blake answered his phone and walked off into another room to talk.

Among the piles was an envelope. Her name written on it in Tommy's handwriting. She ripped it open and began to read, tears filling her eyes.

Kara, if you got this, it's cause I fucked up. Either I'm inside or I'm dead. If I'm dead, take this cash and get the fuck out of town. Get rid of the tapes, and tell no one you have them. If I'm inside, bring the tapes to my lawyer and bring cash.

Tommy.

She read the letter over again and again, hoping to find more. A sentiment that she could hold onto, to make her feel safe and loved. Nothing. Her brother had left her instructions on how to clean up his mess. No apologies, no words of wisdom on how to get on without him. The tears fell down her cheeks, but no longer from grief.

"Hey, Kara." Blake stood over her, holding out his phone. "It's Devin." Something like pity played in his voice and his eyes when she took the phone.

"Devin?" She wiped her nose and gripped the phone hard.

"Peaches. It's done. You'll be safe now," he said in a clipped tone.

She let out a long breath and wiped her hands across her eyes. It was over with. They could move on now. "Okay. Are you coming for me now?" She glanced at Blake who was still watching her with concern. Like she was going to crumble right before his eyes.

"Blake is going to take you to the police station. They have some questions for you, and I want you to answer everything honestly. Don't hide anything trying to protect me. You tell them everything if you want about what we did up at the farmhouse."

Did he want her to press charges on him? She forced a laugh. "I don't think they'll arrest you for spanking me, Devin." She stood from the couch, giving Blake her back. "I don't want to press charges, just come get me."

"Kara, go with Blake. Do what he says, and what the cops say. In your purse—"

"The money. I saw." She gripped the cell harder, feeling

the edges bite into her fingers and not caring.

"You have to go, away from the city. They'll help you get set up somewhere. Blake will help—"

"What about you?" She whispered her question, pressing her forehead against the window, feeling the thick fabric of the curtains rub against her forehead.

"And no more internet searches. Blake will give you some places you can go, you know, to explore—but none of that online shit."

"Devin." Her voice cracked and she tried again. "You'll come back, right? I mean, you said—"

"I can't keep you, pet. It wouldn't be right. What I did—it wasn't right."

Fat, hot tears rolled down her cheeks. Wasn't right? Everything about them felt right, perfect. What was he blathering on about? He was dumping her off on Blake, who was going to dump her at the police station.

Her mind reeled. "I don't understand. You said what we did—there was no shame. Those were your words. That's what you told me. You—"

"I'm an undercover FBI agent, Kara!" He'd never raised his voice at her before, not like that, not with such impatience. "I've been working undercover in Michael Cardone's crew for the past two years. When your brother was brought up to Captain, I was put on his crew. I knew everything about you in just a few weeks. After he was murdered, I went through your apartment. I went through your computer, your closets, everything. There wasn't a part of you I didn't know."

She didn't know how to react. Too much information in too short a time. "You went through my computer?"

He sighed, a heaviness that spoke of sadness. "When Michael gave the order to snag you, to find whatever Tommy had left behind, I took the job. To protect you."

"Why didn't you tell me? Why didn't you just tell me?" Anger started to simmer. Had anything between them been real?

"Michael's always been paranoid, I couldn't chance that I wasn't being watched. I had to snag you and get out of town, make it look like I was doing what I was supposed to do."

"When we were alone—you could have told me then!"

"I know, but by then things between us, they had escalated."

"It was all a lie?" She wanted him to be there with her, right in front of her so she could see the betrayal in his eyes.

"No. Not everything. Not us. My job, I didn't tell you what my job was, but everything else was real, peaches. Completely real."

"But you aren't coming back." She inhaled slowly, trying to calm her heart and keep her cool. "Everything we did was real, everything you said to me was the truth—except for your job—but you can't come back?"

"I can't keep you," he said in a pained whisper.

She clenched her eyes, straightened her back, and lifted her chin. One swipe across her face and she wiped away the tears. "Well, who the hell asked you to?" Her thumb hit the end call button before he could respond.

She held the phone in her hand for several moments before shaking her head and turning back to Blake. His eyes were soft, but she raised her hand. "I'm fine," she assured him.

"We should go. The sooner—"

"I'm not going."

"Devin said—"

"Devin said a lot of things." Like everything would be fine. But how could that be if he wasn't coming back for her?

"There's a protocol—"

She clenched her teeth to keep from screaming. "I don't fucking care. Either take me to the train station, or at least stay out of my way while I go." She tossed his phone on the couch and grabbed her purse.

"Okay. Okay." He swiped his keys from the bowl near

the front door and went back for his phone. "It's not what you think, Kara. Devin—"

"I don't care." She lied. She did more than care.

A strong hand gripped her arm and spun her to look at him. A darkness settled in his eyes.

"I'll take you to the train station, but you'll listen to everything I have to say on the way there."

She tried to pull away, but his monkey grip was too strong. "Fine," she agreed.

Blake drove an SUV, probably because it was the only car able to carry his massive bulk. Did the man do anything other than work out?

She listened dutifully as they drove, only hearing half of what he was saying to her. Thoughts of Devin kept her occupied. He'd left her, just dumped her off on a doorstep and left. Her chest ached so badly, she started to rub it with her hand.

"He was protecting you," Blake said again. It seemed to be his mantra for the ride. "I don't know what happened up there, but I know everything he did was to protect you."

"He's not coming back, Blake. There's no need to try to talk him up." She was getting tired from keeping her calm. She needed to get away from Blake, from anything having to do with Devin.

"If he's not coming back, it's because he thinks he's doing the right thing. He's trying to do what's best for you."

"Then he's as much an idiot as he is a liar," she snapped. Her head was starting to pound.

"It's a lot to take in. Just understand that Devin has never, not once in all the years I've known him, been dishonest or malicious."

She didn't respond. There would be no point. Blake was going to side with Devin, and really there weren't sides. Devin had taken those away. She'd been an idiot, a fool for thinking anything had changed, that something more tangible had started to bloom between them.

"Kara, take this." Blake handed her a cell phone. "I have

the number programmed into my phone, and the number for me is in there."

They were parked outside Union Station, but she didn't remember him pulling over. She took the phone with a nod.

"When you settle, call me, text me, whatever, just let me know you're good."

"I'm good now." She tried to give a smile, but knew she failed because he looked more concerned than ever. "I'm a big girl, Blake. I'll take care of myself. It's what I do." With that she opened the door and hopped out.

The blaring of a car horn cut off whatever else he was trying to say to her, so she waved and ran off into the building. Once the heavy door shut behind her, she looked around for the signs for Amtrak.

Out of the city first and foremost. A hotel bed and wine. A lot of wine.

Finding the signs leading the way, she took a deep breath and headed to the ticket counter. Breathing would come easier once she was on the train. Her heart would slow down, and she could feel human again. It would pass, this pain. It would pass.

She choked back a sob as she stepped up to the window.

CHAPTER SIXTEEN

Six months later

"You're a fucking asshole. You know that, right." Blake's hard voice crackled in Devin's earpiece.

Another hundred miles and he'd be there. "Yes. I'm aware. You've told me several times already." He changed lanes to get around a semi-truck driving under the limit.

"You had everything and just tossed it out."

"Yep. We had that conversation, but thanks for the recap. Now. You're sure you got the address right this time? 'Cause I scared the shit out of that little girl in Detroit. I'd rather not have a repeat."

"The address is right. She moved again, but same job, same town. Just new apartment. You should have trained her about staying under the radar. She sucks at it. She's using her credit cards again."

"I'll talk with her about it." Right after several other conversations. "No one but you is looking for her, though. Right? You're sure?"

"I shouldn't even be helping you," Blake said for the tenth time since Devin had called him up.

Two weeks. Devin had lasted two weeks before he went

searching. But Blake had only dropped her at the train station. He didn't find out where she was headed.

He tried to focus on his retirement plan. He told himself he'd done the right thing, putting space between them. So, he put all of his energy into getting everything set up for the grand opening, but every time he walked down into his playroom he would find himself standing in the door of her cage. The pillows were still there, still smelled like her.

"You're helping me because you know she belongs to me."

"You didn't see her; you didn't see that girl's heart break like I did. Her face—fuck, man, I can still see it." Blake had described that moment in detail several times. Kara never could hide anything in her features, and it didn't take too much of his imagination to picture it.

"I know." Devin clenched his teeth. "Just tell me the address is right."

"It's right."

"She still didn't respond?"

"I told you she didn't. Nothing. Not a fucking peep in months." Kara had shot Blake a text letting him know she'd landed, but never responded when he inquired as to where. Or any other text Blake or Devin sent. "Let me know what happens. Good luck, man."

His exit came up, and Devin turned on his signal.

• • • • • • •

The last patient checked out, taking with him his prescriptions and his appointment card. Kara finished tallying up the deposit and placed the cash in her boss's drawer.

Working for the small town doctor wasn't much different than working for Dr. Conrad. Except she didn't have Julie to make the day go by a little faster. She'd been able to get a hold of her, to let her know she was okay, but that was it. Julie didn't understand, and neither did Kara, not really. Her brother had been the one working for a bunch of criminals, yet she was the one living in hiding.

After Devin abandoned her, she spent days piecing together everything. The truth of who her brother really was had been a large pill to swallow. A son of a bitch pimp and drug dealer. Finally getting the courage to find out what she could, she'd done some digging and found the list of arrests.

What threw her for the biggest loop was the bomb Devin dropped on her. Devin Singer was FBI.

Tommy was stupid on top of being a criminal. Michael figured him for a rat, and found a recorder on him once. Everything that was done to him was because of that one tape. Devin had been sent to take care of Kara. For Michael that meant get the tapes and make her disappear. For the FBI that had meant recover the tapes and keep her safe from Michael.

All of that was in the past now. She had her future to look forward to. A new job, a new town, a new apartment. Things were going to be okay; well, at least steady.

Devin popped into her mind now and again. She couldn't stop him from invading her thoughts or her dreams any more than she'd been able to keep him from making her soften in his arms. She couldn't stay angry at him for lying about being undercover. Devin didn't do anything without reason, his keeping that part of him a secret was his way of keeping her safe. Much the same way Tommy had. The less she knew, the better.

The abandonment ate at her. He'd opened her eyes to so much, and then he'd just left her. Just walked away after all his lessons in obedience and making her believe she could trust him, could let him take care of her. All for what? He fucking left her.

She finished closing up the office and headed home. She walked most nights. The spring air did her good to clear her thoughts on the way home. She lived in a three-level again; this time she had taken the middle floor apartment.

Mrs. Watersby sat on the front porch when she got

home, reading the newspaper. The older woman waved to Kara, as she walked past to get inside. Her head hurt and her feet were sore. She wanted to eat something quick and lie on the couch. Staring off into the television set sounded perfect.

She hadn't gone back to her old apartment for anything. There wasn't anything for her to claim. She picked up a new laptop and furniture, all with the dirty money her brother left behind. The cash she always turned down now bought her clothes and food.

After changing out of her scrubs and into her pajamas, she sank into her couch, eyeing the laptop on the coffee table. She hadn't frequented any of the chat rooms that she used to lurk in before Devin. There was no point. She'd had exactly what she wanted, and it dropped her on her head. She wasn't going to do that again. She took the hint. Alone worked better.

The frozen pizza worked fine for dinner, and she threw on Netflix, flipping through until she found something worth watching. Nothing was worth watching, not really, but the background noise gave her a sense of life. When it was silent was when her mind would start racing toward the memory of those dark eyes. The harsh hands. The bite of the flogger, the belt, and even the strap. All of those put together didn't compare to the bite of his rejection. His abandonment.

"Fuck him," she growled to herself and turned the volume up higher.

• • • • • • •

A hand covered her mouth, startling her awake. She tried to jump up, to sit up in her bed, but the hand clamped down harder, pushing her to her mattress. Her eyes flew open, searching for the person, but it was too dark, her blinds were closed, all lights were off in the apartment.

"You left the front door unlocked, peaches." That voice.

The sound of that voice brought tears to her eyes immediately.

She shoved at him, but he didn't relent in his hold on her. "Now, now, no struggling. You know I'll win. I'm going to let go of your mouth, but you aren't going to scream. You're going to sit up and turn on your nightstand light. Do you understand, peaches?"

Her jaw tightened. Biting him sounded like a good idea, but she nodded instead.

"That's a good girl." He rolled his hand away from her mouth and she flew off the bed, pulling the string of the light until it burned brightly.

It was him. Devin stood not five feet from her in his black t-shirt and jeans. His hair had grown a bit, but otherwise he was the same. Exactly the same. Taller maybe? Did he always look that big? Her tongue thickened in her mouth; any questions she had for him were trapped.

"I know you're pissed," he offered. Pissed? She passed pissed five months ago. Tortured would be more accurate.

"Why are you here?" she managed, folding her arms over her stomach.

He shrugged and let out a heavy sigh. "I couldn't do it."

"Do what?" The ache in her chest grew with the pounding of her heart.

"I couldn't keep you, but I couldn't let you go, either." He sank onto the bed, not reaching for her, or demanding she go to him. "I tried. Damn, did I try." He raked his hand through his hair. "I shouldn't have left you. I should have stayed."

"But you didn't. You left," she shrugged, not giving him an inch. Not yet. Not when the tears were still brimming in her eyes, and her hands wanted nothing more than to touch him to be sure he was real.

"I was trying to do the right thing. What we had, it was intense, more real than anything I'd experienced before. But the situation, the way we came together, it wasn't right."

"You told me once that nothing I did with you was

shameful, that everything we did was good." She thrust her chin up.

"You didn't lock your door. You didn't change your name. You didn't even change your career." Back to the dominating protector.

"What do you want, Devin?" She leaned against the wall. Her legs were having trouble keeping her upright with him so close.

He got off the bed, took two strides to get to her, and trapped her against the wall with his hands on either side of her face. So close, she could smell him. The musky smell of him. A tear fell, but she didn't wipe it away; maybe he wouldn't notice it if she didn't draw attention.

His lips caught it just as it reached her chin, and he kissed her cheek. "Don't cry, peaches. I'm here now. I'm sorry. I'm sorry I left you."

"I was your job. That's all, I got it." She didn't get anything, at least not at first. It took a long time for her to sort out what had happened between them, what was real and what wasn't. He worked for the FBI, but nothing else about what took place in that farmhouse was secret to her. She could feel every lash he gave her, every kiss, every caress. None of that had been fabricated, none of it would leave her memory even when she wanted it to.

"At first, yeah. My job. Keep you safe, get those tapes, turn them over, and take down the Cardone family. But you ran away. You escaped, then you tried to kill me, and then you took every punishment, every lesson, every bit of pain and bliss I gave you and you did it with an honesty that I'd never seen before. You weren't surviving a kidnapping; you were finding yourself." Way to hit the nail on the head, six months later. "You weren't scared of me. Even when you thought that I might actually kill you, you weren't afraid. You feared punishment, but not me. Never me."

"So?" Could her voice crack any more? She couldn't sound so frail, not when she'd worked so tiredly to harden herself against him.

"You stopped being a job the moment I had that collar around your neck." The memory of him taking the collar off her, taking it from her, started a whole new ache. "You were mine then. I knew it. Fuck, Trevor knew it. You know how much shit he gave me about having that collar on you?"

"My hero." She'd have to give him a nice thank you the next she saw the betraying prick. "So, you're here." It occurred to her to push him away. Having him so close made it harder to think.

"I'm here," he nodded. "For you."

It was her turn to laugh. "I'm not going anywhere with you, Devin."

His grin, the evil smile she remembered vividly from that first night, appeared. "Has my pet forgotten the rules? You have one choice to make, peaches, just one. What is it?"

She swallowed. She couldn't do it, not again. "You'll just leave me again. It's what people do, Devin, they leave me."

"I was a fucking idiot to leave you. I've been a complete asshole since I left you at Blake's. He's pissed as hell at me, if that helps you. Took some convincing to get his help to track you down to this place."

"I'm doing fine, Devin. I have a job. I have an apartment. Give me a few more years, I might actually make a friend."

He moved one hand from the wall to cup her chin. "Come home with me, pet."

"Home with you?" His lips were so close, just a hair more and she could taste him. "You left me."

"And I'll spend the rest of our lives making up for it." A stronger vow she had never heard. "I was an ass. I should have told you, should have been telling you every fucking day."

Hope clung to her, but she had to know. "Tell me what?"

His tongue wet his lips and he took a deep breath. "I love you, Kara. Probably since the first time I saw you. I love you."

She covered her mouth with her fingers; the empowerment of three words was never so great as with those exact words.

"I tried to find you," she breathed out, dropping her hand. "I drove up and down that damn highway trying to remember the exit. Got lost a few times." Three to be exact. Too many winding country roads and not enough streetlamps.

"You shouldn't have done that. What if you had gotten in trouble? You never answered any of Blake's texts, or mine, how would we have found you?"

"I tossed that cell phone," she admitted, somewhat enjoying the frustration building in his gaze.

"Peaches," he sighed, pressing his forehead against hers. "I'm going to forget that. I'll just chalk it up to my fault for letting you run wild." He nuzzled his nose against her cheek.

"Will you let me strap you?" she asked on a whim.

He pulled back as though she'd slapped him, and his jaw tensed. "Would that make it better?"

The picture of him tied to that tree behind the farmhouse popped into her mind, and she had to shake her head. "No. There can be only one of us that holds the strap." The corner of his mouth turned upward.

"Then you should probably pack your clothes. One bag, fifteen minutes." He pushed off the wall and pulled out his phone. After a few taps on the screen he turned it to her. The timer started ticking down. "Fifteen minutes. If you aren't in the living room with your bag by the time this goes off, we'll start our new life off with a spanking."

If he hadn't winked on his way to the closet, she might have been nervous. He was back. He came back for her.

CHAPTER SEVENTEEN

A soft summer breeze blew through the trees, making the branches and leaves dance. Beneath the whispering willow, on a plush blanket in the shade, Kara slept. Dark, angry welts crossed her bare ass and down her thighs, and several red blotches covered her naked back, but peacefully she slept.

Devin watched her breathing from the deck. She'd taken her caning so well, with such open submission, he'd rewarded her with a flogging. To anyone outside of their world, it would make little sense that she would seek something like the feel of a heavy flogger against her bare back only hours after taking a severe punishment. But to his Kara, his pet, the flogging completed the day.

They'd been back at his farmhouse for nearly a year. The construction was complete, and his retirement in full swing. It had shocked her the day he brought her back to the farmhouse, after taking the biggest risk of his life with sneaking into her apartment. He'd been shaking beneath his skin that night, worried she wouldn't or couldn't forgive him for his stupidity. She'd teased him about taking a strap for his punishment. He would have. He would have done everything in his power to make sure she understood how much he regretted running away.

The case had closed, the need for him to testify didn't even exist thanks to Tommy's tapes. No one, other than Jason, knew he had anything to do with the tapes. The last tape Tommy recorded before he'd been caught by Michael wasn't a conversation. Just Tommy laying out everything he'd done, and everything he'd discussed with Devin. If that tape fell into the wrong hands, it could have caused a whole mess of trouble for him. Jason may have been able to look the other way when his brother and his crew were taken down, but if he had proof that Devin had been undercover, that the feds had been able to wiggle someone into their family undetected, it would have been the end for Devin. As it happened, from what he could see in the papers, and what contacts he still kept in touch with at the bureau, Jason took to being the boss with complete ease. Making more money than ever.

Kara came home with him that night, but it took a lot of time to get her back. She was cautious and standoffish at first, and he brought her back around to him with more patience than the first time around. He needed to prove himself, and he worked his ass off to do it.

Together they finished the farmhouse and all of the cabins. By the end of six months together, the Tryst Resort was open for business. They'd hired a small staff of personnel to work the cleaning crews and hospitality departments, but Devin took care of all guest vetting himself. The safe haven for couples wanting to get away and play to their hearts' content with no judgment had opened. Reservations were booked for three months out. Kara had thought him crazy when he explained that the cabins were built for the guests, but the barn was a fully equipped dungeon that would be open to the guests full time. He had security staff working as dungeon monitors during the heaviest time when play took place, and security cameras took their place during the other times. Always being monitored by a security member.

Originally he intended the farmhouse to be a B&B, but after bringing Kara back, he realized he didn't want to share the house with anyone. The spare bedrooms became VIP rooms, for his close friends and his brother when he popped in, but they weren't for regular guests.

After two months of living with him, Kara had come across her collar. Not by mistake, he'd left it out on the dresser one morning. She'd brought it to him at the breakfast table, knelt in front of him, and asked him if he would put it back on. He'd said no and presented her with a permanent one, a silver band that had a concealed lock to which he held the key. No pomp and circumstance was needed. Not between them. He snapped it in place and she'd jumped, naked as how he kept her these days, into his lap, hugging him tightly.

That's not to say she didn't still spout off at the mouth and get her attitude riled. But when she did, when she left her place, he was there. Always there, just like he promised, to put her back in the spot she found comforting, and loved.

"Sir? The crew would like to set up for the collaring ceremony we have scheduled this evening." Maria, in charge of guest events, joined him on the deck and motioned to where his pet napped.

He looked at his watch. "She's napped long enough. I'll take her in the house." He waved, jogging down the few steps to the grass and walked over to her, still watching her breathing, and enjoying the sight of his mark on her back and ass.

"Peaches. You have to get up, babe." He squatted down at her side and gently stroked her arm. She murmured something to him, but he couldn't understand. "You have to get up. I'll carry you if you want, but then I'm putting you in your cage." She didn't hate the cage anymore; in fact, she took most of her naps in there when he was busy with his day. She didn't care for it when she was put there for restriction, but otherwise she enjoyed the time of seclusion.

"Fine," she mumbled and moved to stand. He helped

her to her feet, took one look at the sleepy look in her eyes, and scooped her into his arms.

"You didn't sleep enough last night. No more reading when I go to sleep. Book down at midnight." She wrapped her arms around his neck and only winced when his hand brushed one of her welts.

"Fine."

"I hate that word, pet, and I thought you would have learned your lesson about your mouth this morning." He put more pressure on her ass, and she yelped.

"I'm sorry, Sir." She snuggled into his chest. "Do I have to go to my cage?"

The whispered question was placed against his neck. "Do you want to go to your cage, or would you rather go to bed? With me?"

"With you, always with you." She held him tighter.

He carried her down to his personal play area, bypassing the cage and placing her on the bed. He sat beside her, stroking her cheek as she looked up at him with desire. He'd given her the flogging for her reward, but he hadn't fucked her. Not yet, and not on a day she'd earned a caning. The woman would learn to keep her mouth in check. Maybe someday. Not too soon, though, he hoped.

"I've decided something." He kissed the tip of her nose. She wiggled on the bed, trying to find a spot that wasn't sore to touch, and not finding one. He was a thorough disciplinarian. Especially when his pet called him names and cursed at him because she didn't agree with something he said. "I've decided we are going to get married."

She laughed, a soft sound. "Oh, you did? Don't you think that's something you should ask me? I mean, it's usually the way it's done."

"Did I ask you when I took you from your apartment, or when I made you my pet here in this room, or when I put this collar around you?"

After taking a second to think it over, she said, "No. You didn't, but maybe this one time could be normal?" She reached up to touch his face. The feather touch of her fingers always worked to soften his resolve.

"Nothing about you is normal. You are the most extraordinary woman I have ever met. When you should have buckled beneath the pressure of life, you thrived. When you should have been searching out help, you were taking responsibility for others. So no. I've decided. And the only choice you have to make is what?" He hovered closer to her face, within a breath of touching her lips. Wanting nothing more than to take her at that moment.

"To obey or not obey you, Sir." The whispered answer came right before a tear slid down her cheek. He knew her well enough to know when she was stressed or when she was happy. He kissed the tear away, taking her happiness into his soul.

"That's right, peaches. Be my wife. Make me the happiest son of a bitch for the rest of our lives. I don't deserve it, but do it anyway. Not just because I say so, but because it's what you want."

She cupped his face, bringing his eyes to focus on hers. "I want nothing more than to belong to you forever. Your pet, your submissive, your wife. All of it. In every way."

"That's my good girl."

He'd managed the impossible. They both had. In a world where they'd experienced loneliness and sorrow, they found each other. And no matter what life would throw their way from that moment on, she would forever belong to him, and he would forever be her protector. Protector of her heart, her soul, her submission. Everything.

They would everything for each other. Forever.

THE END

STORMY NIGHT PUBLICATIONS WOULD LIKE TO THANK YOU FOR YOUR INTEREST IN OUR BOOKS.

If you liked this book (or even if you didn't), we would really appreciate you leaving a review on the site where you purchased it. Reviews provide useful feedback for us and for our authors, and this feedback (both positive comments and constructive criticism) allows us to work even harder to make sure we provide the content our customers want to read.

If you would like to check out more books from Stormy Night Publications, if you want to learn more about our company, or if you would like to join our mailing list, please visit our website at:

www.stormynightpublications.com

Made in the USA
Monee, IL
22 February 2021